Praise for *Bridget Jones*: *Mad About the Boy*

'Laugh out loud funny.'
Financial Times

'With *Bridget Jones's Diary*, Helen Fielding created
a new female archetype. Now she's brought Bridget
back to conquer the twenty-first century.'
Time

'Fielding has somehow pulled off the neat
trick . . . of allowing her heroine to grow up into
someone funnier and more interesting than before.'
New York Times Book Review

'Inimitable . . . If you don't shed a few tears in the
course of this book, you must have a heart of ice.'
Guardian

'Feels like visiting with your funniest friend.'
Entertainment Weekly

'Fielding's comic gifts – and, just as important,
her almost anthropological ability to nose out all
that is trendy and potentially crazy making
about contemporary culture – are once again
on shimmering exhibit.'
Elle

Bridget Jones's Baby

The Diaries

Based on the columns first published
in the *Independent* newspaper.
With thanks to Working Title Films
and Universal Pictures.

Bridget Jones's Baby

The Diaries

Helen Fielding

JONATHAN CAPE
LONDON

1 3 5 7 9 10 8 6 4 2

Jonathan Cape, an imprint of Vintage Publishing,
20 Vauxhall Bridge Road,
London SW1V 2SA

Jonathan Cape is part of the Penguin Random House group of companies
whose addresses can be found at global.penguinrandomhouse.com.

Penguin
Random House
UK

First published in the United Kingdom by Jonathan Cape in 2016

penguin.co.uk/vintage

A CIP catalogue record for this book is available from the British Library

Hardback ISBN 9781911214564

Printed and bound in Great Britain by Clays Ltd, St Ives PLC

Penguin Random House is committed to a sustainable future
for our business, our readers and our planet. This book is made
from Forest Stewardship Council® certified paper.

For Kevin, Dash and Romy

Contents

Contents

BRIDGET JONES'S BABY

THE DIARIES

INTRO

Dearest Billy,

I have a feeling that you're going to find out about all this, so I thought you'd better hear how it all began, from your own mum.

These are the excerpts from my diaries and other bits and pieces from that rather confused time.

Please don't be shocked. Hopefully you'll be old enough by the time you read them to understand that even your parents got up to this sort of thing, and you know I've always been a bit naughty.

The thing is, just as there is a big gap between how people think they are supposed to be and how they actually are, there's also a gap between how people expect their lives to turn out and how they actually do.

But if you just keep calm and keep your spirits up, things have a habit of turning out all right – just as they did for me, because having you was the best thing that ever happened to me.

Sorry about all this and everything.

Love, Mum x
(Bridget)

ONE

THE MULTIFACETED PORTENT

Noon. London: my flat. Oh God. Oh God. Am beyond late and hung-over and everything is absolutely terrib— Oooh, goody! Telephone!

'Oh, hello, darling, guess what?' – my mother. 'We've just been at Mavis Enderbury's Brunch Time Karaoke and guess what? Julie Enderbury's just had her . . .'

You could practically hear the screeching of tyres: like she was about to say the word 'fat' to a morbidly obese person.

'Just had her what?' I muttered, frantically putting the remains of a slice of goat's cheese log in my mouth followed by half a protein bar to ease the hangover, whilst trying to pull some sort of vaguely christening-friendly outfit from the mess all over the bed.

'Nothing, darling!' she trilled.

'What has Julie Enderbury just had?' I retched. 'Her boobs made even more gigantic? A lithe young Brazilian?'

'Oh, nothing, nothing, darling. She just had her third, but what I was really ringing to say was . . .'

Grrr! Why does my mother always DO this? It's bad enough *anyway* careering towards baby deadline without . . .

'Why are you avoiding the subject of Julie Enderbury's third?' I rasped, jabbing wildly at the TV remotes for some sort of escape, only to ping up an advert showing an anorexic teenage model with a baby playing with a toilet roll.

'Oh, I'm not, darling,' Mum replied airily. 'Anyway, look at this Angelina Jolly. She adopted that Chinese baby . . .'

'I think you'll find Maddox was Cambodian, Mother,' I said, coldly. Honestly, the way she talks about celebrities you'd think she'd just had an intimate conversation with Angelina Jolie at Mavis Enderbury's Brunch Time Karaoke.

'The point is, Angelina adopted this little baby and then she got Brad, and had all these other babies.'

'I don't think that's why Angelina "got" Brad Pitt, Mother. Having a baby is not the be all and end all of a woman's life,' I said, struggling into an absurd floaty peach dress, which I last wore at Magda's wedding.

'That's the spirit, darling. And some people have marvellous lives without them! Look at Wynn and Ashley Green! They went down the Nile thirty-four times! Mind you, they were a couple, so . . .'

'Actually, Mum, for once in my life, I'm very happy. I'm successful, I have a new car with satnav and I'm freeee . . .' I gushed, glancing out of the window to see – bizarrely – a group of pregnant women walking along the road below the flat, fondling their bumps.

'Hmmm. Anyway, darling. You'll never guess what?'

'What?'

There were three more pregnant women walking along behind the first lot now. It was starting to get weird.

8

'She's accepted! The Queen! She's doing a Royal Visit on March twenty-third to celebrate the fifteen-hundredth anniversary of the Ethelred Stone.'

'What? Who? Ethelred?'

A veritable throng of pregnant women was now walking along the street below.

'You know? That thing in the village by the fire hydrant where Mavis got her car clamped. It's Anglo-Saxon,' Mum autowittered on. 'Anyway, aren't you supposed to be at the christening today? Elaine told me Mar—'

'Mum. Something very strange is happening,' I said eerily. 'Gotogobye.'

Grrr! Why does everyone try to make you feel stupid about not having babies? I mean, pretty much everybody feels an element of ambivalence about the whole thing, including my mother. She's always saying, 'Sometimes I wish I'd never HAD children, darling.' And anyway, it's not that easy to pull off in the modern world, as men are an increasingly unevolved primitive species, and the last thing you want is . . . Gaah! Doorbell.

12.30 p.m. Was Shazzer – finally! Buzzed her in, then darted, freaked-out, back to the window, whilst she clopped across the room to the fridge, dressed in a wildly christening-inappropriate little black dress and Jimmy Choos.

'Bridge, come the fuck ON. We're beyond late! Why are you hiding under the window dressed like a fairy?'

'It's an omen,' I gabbled. 'God is punishing me for

being a selfish career woman and thwarting nature with contraceptive devices.'

'What are you the fuck on about?' she said cheerfully, opening the fridge. 'Have you got any wine?'

'Didn't you see? The street is full of pregnant women. It's a multifaceted portent. Soon cows will be falling from the sky, horses born with eight legs and . . .'

Shazzer wandered over to the window and glanced out, pert bum tightly encased in the little black dress.

'There's nobody down there except one vaguely hot boy with a beard. Though actually not hot. Well, not very. Maybe without the beard.'

I leapt up to the window and stared down at the empty street in confusion. 'They're gone. Gone. But where?'

'OK, calm, calm, lovely calm, calm,' said Shazzer, with the air of an American cop talking to her eighth gun-toting lunatic that day. I blinked at her, like a rabbit caught in headlights, then bolted out of the door and down the stairs, hearing her clattering behind me.

Hah! I thought, once out in the street. There were TWO MORE of the pregnant women, hurrying along in the same direction.

'Who are you?' I boldly confronted them. 'What is the meaning of you? Where are you bound?'

The women pointed to a sign outside the closed-down vegan cafe. It said POP-UP PREGNANCY YOGA.

Heard Shazzer snort behind me.

'Right, excellent, jolly good,' I said to the women. 'Have a lovely, lovely, afternoon.'

'Bridget,' said Shaz, 'you are so insane.' Then we both collapsed in slightly hysterical giggles on the doorstep.

1.04 p.m. My car. London. 'It's fine, we'll be early,' said Shazzer.

It was four minutes after we were supposed to be at the pre-christening drinks at Chislewood House and we were in solid traffic on the Cromwell Road. But in my new car, which you can tell to take you to places and make phone calls and everything.

'Call Magda,' I said smoothly to the car.

'You said, Courmayeur,' replied the car.

'No, not Courmayeur, fuckwit,' yelled Shazzer.

'Diverting to Flintwick,' said the car.

'No! You stupid trollop,' yelled Shazzer.

'Diverting to Studely Wallop.'

'Don't shout at my car.'

'What, you're sticking the fuck up for your car now?'

'Put your knickers on. Put them ON,' Magda's voice suddenly boomed out from the car. 'You are NOT coming to a christening without knickers.'

'We are wearing knickers!' I said indignantly.

'Speak for yourself,' murmured Shaz.

'Bridget! Where are you? You're the godmother. Mummy will smack, she will smack, she will smack.'

'It's fine! We're speeding through the countryside! We'll be there any minute!' I said, glancing giddily at Shazzer.

'Oh good, well hurry up we need drinkies first to fortify us. Actually, there's something I wanted to tell you.'

'What?' I said, relieved that Magda wasn't completely furious. It was all turning into a jolly day out.

'Um, it's about the other godparent.'

'Yeees?'

'Look, I'm really sorry. We've had so many kids we've completely run out of any remotely solvent males. Jeremy asked him without telling me.'

'Asked who?'

There was a pause with screaming in the background. Then a single word cut me like a French cook's knife through goat's cheese.

'Mark.'

'You are joking,' said Shazzer.

Silence.

'No, seriously, you are joking, Magda?' said Shazzer. 'What the fuck, fuck are you fucking doing, you masochistic maniac? You are not making her stand at the fucking font with Mark Darcy, in front of a fucking smug married/smug motherfucking—'

'Constance! Put it back. BACK IN THE TOILET! Sorry, got to go!'

The phone cut out.

'Stop the car,' said Shaz. 'We're not going. Turn round.'

'Take the next. Legal. U-turn,' said the car.

'Just because Magda is so desperate to hang on to Jeremy she's had an "accidental" late baby and therefore run out of godparents, there's no reason to have you playing mummies and daddies at the altar with your anally retentive ex.'

12

'But I have to go. It's my duty. I'm the godmother. People go to Afghanistan.'

'Bridget, this is not Afghanistan, it's a ridiculous, tired, social clusterfuck. Pull over.'

I tried to pull over, but everyone started hysterically honking. Eventually I found a petrol station attached to Sainsbury's Homebase.

'Bridge.' Shazzer looked at me and brushed a bit of hair away from my face. For a moment I thought maybe she was a lesbian.

I mean, young people apparently don't see themselves as either gay or straight now, they just ARE: and also women are so much easier to relate to than men. But then I like having sex with men, and I've never . . .

'Bridget!' said Shazzer sternly. 'You've gone into a trance again. You spend your whole time doing what everyone else wants. Get what you need. Get some sex. If you're hell-bent on going to this fucked-up night-mare, get some sex AT THE NIGHTMARE. That's exactly what I'm going to do, not at the nightmare, but in my flat, and if you're determined to put your-self in a COMPLETELY UNACCEPTABLE situation to please everyone else I'm going to get in a cab. I, for one, am going to spend the afternoon christening my toy boy.'

But Magda is my friend and has always been kind. So I drove to the christening having a pity party about what might have been, all alone apart from my new car, which was fortunately feeling quite chatty.

Five Years Before

I still can't believe what happened. I didn't mean to do anything wrong. I was just trying to be nice. Shazzer is right. I must go back and do more reading: e.g., *Why Men Love Bitches*.

Mark and I had our engagement party in Claridge's Ballroom. I'd rather have had it somewhere a bit more bohemian, with fairy lights, baskets instead of lampshades, sofas outside that are meant to be inside, etc. But Claridge's is the sort of place Mark thinks is right for engagements, and that's the point in relationships, you have to adapt. And Mark, who cannot sing, *sang*. He had rewritten the words to 'My Funny Valentine'.

My funny valentine, sweet funny valentine,
You've set my frozen heart to 'thaw',
Though your talk is hardly erudite,
Of calories and cellulite,
With each flaw I endure I love you more.
You're obsessed about your weight. Pathologically late.
Permanently in a state of disarray.
But don't start reading Proust and Poe.
OK!'s OK and so's *Hello!*.
All I want's your warmth and honesty.
Don't change at all, just marry me.

He couldn't really sing, but he's normally so buttoned up that everyone was quite emotional and Mark lost all control and kissed me on the lips at a public occasion. I honestly thought I'd never be so happy again in my entire life.

Later, indeed, things went rather dramatically downhill.

Resolutions

If anything ever almost works out again I will not have anything to do with either of the following:

a) Karaoke
b) Daniel Cleaver (my ex-boyfriend, Mark Darcy's arch rival, old friend from Cambridge, and also the person who broke up Mark's first marriage by being on Mark's kitchen table, having sex with Mark's first wife at the moment when Mark came home from work)

I was just stumbling down from one of the tables, after my rendition of 'I Will Always Love You', when I noticed Daniel Cleaver looking at me with a haunted, tragic expression.

The thing about Daniel is that he *is* very manipulative and sexually incontinent, and unfaithful and does tell a lot of lies, and can be very unkind, and obviously Mark hates him because of everything that happened in the past, but I do still think there is something really lovely about him.

'Jones,' said Daniel. 'Help me? I am tortured by regret. You're the only living creature who could possibly, ever have saved me and now you are marrying another. I find myself disintegrating, almost as if falling to pieces. Just a few kind words alone, Jones, please?'

'Yessuvcourse, Dansyul, coss,' I slurred, confusedly. 'I juss wan' everyone to be as happy assme.' In hindsight, I may have been the teensiest bit drunk.

Daniel was taking my arm and steering me in some sort of direction.

'I am tortured, Jones. I am tormented.'

'No. Lisssten. I really, really sink that . . . happiness is soooo . . .'

'Come in here, Jones, please. I really need to talk, alone . . .' said Daniel, leading me unsteadily into a side room. 'Is my life now doomed, forever, truthfully?'

'No!' I said. 'Snow! Daniel! Yous WILL be happy! Defsnut.'

'Hold me, Jones,' he said. 'I fear I will never . . .'

'Lissen. Happiness IS happy because . . .' I said, as we overbalanced and crashed onto the floor.

'Jones,' he growled, hornily. 'Just let me have one last look at your giant mummy pants I so love. To make Daddy happy? Before my life disintegrates into ashes?'

The door burst open and I looked up in horror to see Mark's face, just as Daniel was lifting up my skirt. There was a flash of pain in Mark's brown eyes, and then total, cold, emotional shutdown.

It was the one thing Mark couldn't forgive. Mark and I left the party together, as if nothing was wrong. For weeks we struggled on, pretending to everyone else that things were OK and trying and failing to pretend to each other.

As you may know, I have a degree in English Language and Literature from Bangor University, and it made me think of a line from one of D. H. Lawrence's marvellous works:

Something in her proud, honourable soul had crystallised out, hard as rock, against him.

Something in Mark's proud, honourable soul had crystallised out against me. 'What the fuck is wrong with him? It was a meaningless moment compared to a whole lifetime. He knows what Daniel's like,' said the friends. But for Mark, it went very deep in a way I couldn't understand and he couldn't explain. It was the straw that broke the camel's back. Eventually, he told me he couldn't carry on. I still had my flat. He apologised for the inconvenience, heartbreak, etc. He orchestrated the spread of the news that the engagement was broken amongst our friends and family in a typically dignified way and shortly afterwards left for a job in Northern California.

The friends were brilliant, ranting, 'He's completely anally retentive, fucked up by public school and will never commit to anyone.' Six months later, he married Natasha the uptight stick-insect lawyer woman who was with Mark the first time I saw him in a suit – at a book party for *Kafka's Motorbike*, where she was going on and on to Salman Rushdie about 'hierarchies of culture', and the only thing I could think of to say was, 'Do you know where the toilets are?'

I never heard back from Daniel. 'FUCK Daniel. He's a sexually incontinent emotional fuckwitted commitment-phobe who'll never commit to anyone,' ranted Shazzer. Seven months later, Daniel married an Eastern European model/princess and was occasionally to be seen gracing the pages of *Hello!*, leaning over the parapet of a castle with mountains in the background, looking slightly embarrassed.

*   *   *

And so, there I was, five years later, crawling along the M4, horrifyingly late, to see Mark again for the first time since it all ended.

Two

The Christening

2.45 p.m. Car park, Nether Stubbly Church, Gloucestershire. OK. Everything is completely fine. Is only fifteen minutes after christening was supposed to commence, and nothing ever starts on time, right? Will be serene, calm and dignified. Will simply ask myself, at any awkward moment, 'What would the Dalai Lama do?' And then do it.

As I climbed out of the car, I entered a beautiful, Cotswold summer scene: an ancient church, roses, the smell of cut grass, the leaves hanging heavy. There was silence, apart from birds and bees. It was beautiful as only England can be, on the annual day when the sun shines, and everyone panics in case it's never going to happen again till the following year.

Started teetering my way towards the church, slightly alarmed that no one was in sight. Surely they couldn't have started the christening without the Godmother? Suddenly, there was the roar of a helicopter. I stood, with my dress and hair billowing, to see the helicopter swoop down. Bond-like, without the helicopter even touching the ground, Mark Darcy leapt out and strode towards the church as the helicopter roared up and away.

Tried to compose self, as far as possible when wearing

21

heels in grass, and got myself into the church in the nick of time. Told myself everything would be completely fine, because had got down to my ideal weight and therefore everyone would see that I had completely changed. Felt a familiar thrill at seeing Mark's tall, upright figure at the font. As I made my way down the aisle, I distinctly heard Cosmo say, 'Is she ill? She looks like a stick insect! What happened to the . . . you know . . . boobs?'

As I approached the font, the vicar said, 'Well! Perhaps now we can make a start!' adding, under his breath, 'I've got another three of these nightmares this afternoon.'

'Bridget, where the fuck were you, where's Shazzer?' hissed Magda, at which her latest christenee, Molly, started screaming. 'Here – take her.' Magda handed the baby over to me – she smelt so yummy of baby powder and milk. Gratifyingly she snuggled in to my boobs – which by the way are STILL THERE – and stopped crying.

Mark acknowledged me with the merest flicker of an eye.

Actually, the christening was fine. Have done it often enough, I *so* have it down. But immediately afterwards, instead of milling around with everyone outside, Mark shot off somewhere and disappeared.

When I got to the party, I blundered straight into a group of Smug Mothers.

'All an Australian nanny does is text.'

'Get an Eastern European! Audrona has a degree in Aeronautical Engineering from the University of Budapest.'

'Oh look here's Bridget!' cooed Mufti. 'Everyone's favourite godmother!'

'How many is it now, Bridget?' said Caroline, stroking her pregnant bump.

'Four hundred and thirty-seven,' I said, brightly. 'Thirty-eight counting this one! Ooh must just go off and—'

'You really should have some of your own, you know, Bridget,' said Woney. 'Time's running out.'

For a second had a vision of myself grabbing Woney by the ears and bellowing, 'Do you think it hasn't crossed my *mind*?' but I didn't because, ironically enough, as so often over the last decade, I didn't want to hurt her feelings.

'Do you want to feel my bump?' said Caroline, stroking her pregnant bump.

'No, not really, thanks.'

'No go on, feel it.'

'No, I really need a—'

'Feel. The bump,' she said, with startling ferocity. 'Oh, she's kicking me!'

'And frankly who can blame her?' Magda steamed in. 'Leave Bridget alone you ghastly grow-bags. You're just wishing you could have jobs and shag lithe young sex gods like she does. Come and get a drink, Bridge.'

She swept me out of the torture chamber, then

suddenly stopped in her tracks, looking ashen, and whispered, 'Jeremy's talking to that woman again.'

'Oh my God, Magda, I'm so sorry. Is he still at it?' I said.

'Yup. I'd better get in there. Bar's over there. Laters.'

Walked through the crush round the bar, straight into a bunch of drunken fathers.

'If you want a shot at Westminster at six, you have to start tutoring at three.'

'Yars. But you've got another crack at eleven.'

'No chance.'

'Not unless they have the Latin.'

'Bridget! Have you been ill? Where are the bloody boobs?'

'Got yourself a boyfriend yet?'

I managed to ease my way through without incident by nodding and smiling enigmatically. Hurled myself at the bar thinking nothing could possibly get worse, and found myself standing next to Mark Darcy.

The conversation went as follows.

MARK DARCY: Hello.
ME: Hello.
MARK DARCY: How are you?
ME: (*strange voice*) I am very well thank you. How are you?
MARK DARCY: I am fine.
ME: So am I.

MARK DARCY: Good.

ME: Yes.

MARK DARCY: Good.

ME: Yes.

MARK DARCY: Well, goodbye then.

ME: Yes. Goodbye, then.

We both turned to separate barmen.

'Glass of white wine, please,' I said.

'Vodka martini,' I heard Mark say.

'Big, big glass.'

'Actually make that a treble.'

'Very big.'

'With a whisky chaser.'

We stood, incredibly awkwardly with our backs to each other. Then, the drunken fathers started on Mark.

'Darcyyyyyyyyyy! How the devil are you, you old bastard? What you doing turning up late like that in a chopper?'

'Well, I was actually, um, in a fairly important Foreign Office meeting.'

The barman handed me the wine, I took a giant slurp and started to make my escape.

'How's single life treating you then, Darcy?' said Cosmo.

I froze. Single life?

'Dark horse, aren't you? Got a new totty yet?'

'Well, I'm hardly . . .' Mark began.

'What's the matter with you, you miserable old sod? Johnny Forrester was barely out of the divorce court before he was inundated with totties. Smothered in them. Out every night.'

Took another huge slurp of wine, just as Mark muttered, 'Yes, I assume you have no idea of the reality of being single at my stage in life. Everywhere you turn, someone's trying to push one at some deluded woman-of-a-certain-age, looking for a knight on a charger to solve all their problems: financial, physical and otherwise. Anyway, must be going. Yup. Must be off.'

Staggered off round a corner and leaned against the wall, mind reeling. Single? Had he split up from Natasha? 'Woman-of-a-certain-age'? Was he talking about ME???? Did he think the christening was some sort of weird set-up? Was he LEAVING? I was bristling with confusion and indignation and on the point of texting Shazzer, when Magda appeared, looking pretty drunk herself now. 'Bridget!' she said. 'Mark is divorced. Divorced! He's left the stick insect.'

'I just heard.'

'We have to go outside and discuss this *immediately*.'

As Magda and I squeezed past the bar, the drunken fathers were still on full autowitter.

'What about Bridget? Never understood why those two didn't get sprogged up.'

'They were together long enough.'

'Was she just too old or did he just not have the soldiers?'

*

Out in the garden, we found a large collection of children, none of whom were climbing trees, playing tag, doing three-legged races, etc., in a childlike manner; all of whom were attached to electronic devices. Magda went storming up to them: 'Zac! Off! Now! I said forty-five minutes.'

'But I HAVEN'T FINISHED THIS LEV-ELLLLLLLLL!'

'Off! Now! All of you!' yelled Magda, drunkenly lunging at the devices.

'It's just SO FUCKING UNFAIR!'

'I'm going to lose my CROWNS!'

'I DON'T CARE ABOUT YOUR EFFING CROWNS – GIVE ME THAT THING!'

Unbridled mayhem broke out.

'QUIET!' roared a voice. 'Potter, Roebuck, stop! Stand in line!'

The boys, startled, obviously thinking they were back at school, stood to attention.

'Right,' said Mark, striding in front of them as if he was in court. 'Disgraceful behaviour. Act like men. Ten times round the lake, all of you. First one back' – he took out his iPhone – 'gets Angry Birds for ten minutes. Off you go. Run. FAST.'

The big boys all tore off like racehorses. The little children all burst into tears.

Mark looked nonplussed for a moment. 'Right. Jolly good,' he said, and headed back into the hotel.

*

Archie, one of my many godchildren, who is three, was standing with his stomach sticking out looking sad, his lower lip wobbling. I went to him. He threw his arms round my neck and I felt something pulling at my hair.

'My twain,' said Archie.

'Your what??' I said, reaching up to my head. Oh shit! There was a toy train attached to my head, engine still whirring, winding my hair into it.

'I'm sorry, I'm sorry.' Archie was crying even more now. 'My Thomas de Tank Engine.'

'It's all right, sweetheart, it's all right,' I said, trying to turn off the train.

'Audrona!' Magda yelled. 'Where in the name of arse are all the fucking nannies?'

'Magda! I've got a train stuck to my head!'

There was mayhem in the foreground, while the older kids were still haring around the lake like dervishes. Eventually, the nannies appeared and took the little ones off upstairs. The bigger ones returned from the lake, exhausted, but not too exhausted for Mark's iPhone. It was hard to watch as they clustered around him. Mark Darcy: commanding respect without seeming to try.

My memories of the rest of the occasion were somewhat confused owing to a limitless alcohol supply. I think there was line dancing. And, later, a group of us, including Mark, were standing on the terrace, many of us leaning on walls for support.

'Blurry electronics,' muttered Magda. 'Blurry Zac and his blurry friends.'

'Never have happened if we'd sent him to public school,' said Jeremy, eyes darting back into the bar where 'that woman' cast him a glance.

'Boarding school? He's seven years old, you bastard,' said Magda.

'Yur. Thassjust cruel. Is blurry barbaric,' I concurred.

'I went at seven,' said Mark abruptly.

'Yur, and look what happened to you,' said Magda.

Feeling I was about to get out of my depth, possibly by falling into a water feature, I lurched off down the steps towards the grounds, nearly breaking my ankle in the process, and sat on a bench overlooking the lake in the moonlight.

'So? Cruel, eh?' said Mark's voice behind me.

'Yes, cruel abandonment,' I said, heart beating wildly.

'You don't think they'd be better off with a bit of discipline, backbone, competition?'

'Well it's all very well if you're a tall alpha male and good at everything, but what about the chubby ones, or the confused ones, or the nutty ones? Who do they have to come home to in the evening who thinks they're special . . .'

Mark sat down next to me.

'. . . and loves them' – he said simply – 'just as they are?'

I looked down, trying to compose myself.

'You have a train in your hair.'

'I am aware of that.'

He reached forwards and extracted the train in one simple movement.

'Anything else in there? What's this . . . cake?'

The old sweet, capable Mark. I so wanted to kiss him.

'It's been a while, hasn't it?' he said.

'Yes. Who are you again?'

'No idea.'

'Me neither,' I said.

'I've known you for forty years and I've completely forgotten your name.'

We giggled – Dad's old Grafton Underwood joke.

As Mark looked at me with those deep, brown, soulful eyes, I asked myself, 'What would the Dalai Lama do in this situation?'

We sprang together like unleashed beasts, and continued in that manner in my hotel room, for the rest of the night.

SUNDAY 25 JUNE

In the morning we were still ravenous for each other but also, crucially, food. There was no getting through to room service.

'I'll go grab us something from the buffet,' said Mark, buttoning up his shirt. 'Don't you dare move.'

As he left the room, I heard a male voice in the corridor,

evidently greeting him. The conversation continued, got more heated, then abruptly ended. Which was odd.

I shrugged it off and snuggled down moonily, still shag-drunk, savouring flashbacks to the night before and arranging myself prettily for Mark's return.

The door opened and he came in with a tray full of orange juice, coffee and chocolate croissants.

'Mmmm, thank you, do come back in,' I said.

But he set down the tray and remained standing.

'What's the matter?'

He started pacing. 'I've made a mistake,' he said.

Mind starting spiralling: horror, doom, pain, vulnerable in nightie and him in his suit. Not this? Not such passion and intimacy, instantly replaced by pain and rejection. Not in my nightie.

'I wasn't thinking. I was carried away with emotion, with the joy of seeing you again. I had way too much to drink. We both did. But we cannot proceed.'

'Proceed? That's a funny way to describe shagging.'

'Bridget,' he said, sitting down on the bed. 'I can't do this. I'm newly divorced. I am not in a fit emotional state to take on a relationship at this point in your life.'

'But I didn't ask you for that.'

'I realise, but the question is undoubtedly there, whether it is verbalised or not. At your age, I simply . . . it would be wrong of me . . . I don't want to use up any more of your childbearing years.'

*

7 p.m. My flat. Oh God, oh God. I actually have reached my sexual sell-by date. Men are no longer attracted to me because I am withered and a barren husk.

7.01 p.m. I'm toxic. I'm emitting man-repellent rays.

7.02 p.m. Right. Pah! I cannot allow emotional matters to influence my professional career. I am a professional producer and I will simply multitask and compartmentalise my brain even if I have slept with, then been rejected by, the love of . . . and anyway I do not care about men any more. Simply my work.

7.03 p.m. Being a woman in her late thirties with no kids is the hardest time for a woman. It's a biological kink which I'm sure will be sorted out in years to come. But for now, it's just torture, the clock ticking louder and louder, men sensing the panic and running for the hills, the sense of time running out – and even if you met someone NOW there still wouldn't be time for the relationship to run its course and a baby to happen in the natural run of things.

7.05 p.m. Babies: yuk. I am a top professional woman. Every woman has her *needs*, which I simply fulfil with adult liaisons, almost French in their elegance.

THREE

MEN ARE LIKE BUSES

6 p.m. *Sit Up Britain* **studios.** 'Get over it,' said Miranda. She was sitting in the studio, surrounded by cameras and giant screens, looking immaculate as usual in the presenter's chair, while I controlled the WHOLE THING from the glass studio control gallery above, talking to her through her earpiece.

'Thirty seconds to air,' said Julian the floor manager.

'I can't believe he'd leave like that and assume I was wanting a relationship and babies,' I whispered into Miranda's feed. 'I feel like such a sad act.'

'What are you *talking about*?' said Miranda, as the soundman shoved the mike up her shirt.

'TEN, nine, EIGHT, seven,' Julian the floor manager began.

'This is *Sit Up Britain*, not Victorian Britain,' said Miranda. 'You hooked up with your ex. So what?'

Gaah! Miranda, unbeknownst to herself, was looming up on the screens all over the studio and indeed the country. 'And anyway, fucking your ex doesn't count.'

'Sorry, missed that cue, yes, we are live,' said Julian the floor manager.

'BONG,' went the headline theme, urgent scuttling news music in the background, implying that *Sit Up Britain* minions were scouring for news, antlike, all over the hot spots of the world, when in fact everyone was just arsing around talking about sex in the office.

'Binge drinking!' chirped Miranda, slightly panicked, then clicking into her crisp newsreader voice. 'A serious threat to our young girls, or just good old-fashioned fun?'

BONG. A clip flashed up of drunken girls falling out of a pub.

'Do you think it's because I'm of a certain age?' I whispered into Miranda's earpiece.

'No, it's because he's an emotional retard!' said Miranda, flashing up on the nation's screens again. 'And now Sir Anthony Hopkins . . .'

'. . . extends his ever-extending range,' I – thinking on my feet – said into her feed.

'. . . extends his ever-extending range,' said Miranda, over a shot of an empty-looking chair where Anthony Hopkins was supposed to be for his 'Hello!' shot.

'. . . through the full range of actoring emotions,' I finished for her desperately.

'. . . through the FULL RANGE of actoring emotions,' Miranda said into the camera.

BONG.

'And finally: What makes men gay? A new finding points to the womb environment.'

'What makes fuckwits fuckwits, more like,' said Miranda, leaning back in her chair, thinking the clip had started when it hadn't, quite.

'Bridget! Miranda!' Richard Finch – my long-time boss – burst into the control room. 'I've told you not to talk between the effing bongs. This is a total fucking shambles, and where's Anthony Hopkins?'

I panicked. 'Shit! Where is he? Where's Anthony Hopkins?' The news clip was ending and there was no Anthony Hopkins.

'Get Anthony Hopkins in the chair,' I rasped into Julian the floor manager's feed.

'And now, fresh from location, our next guest . . .' said Miranda, brightly.

'Spread, Miranda, spread,' I hissed.

I spotted Anthony Hopkins, grey-haired in a suit, wandering distractedly round the studio.

'Julian, he's there, camera left, I mean right, whatever, behind the chair.'

'Knight of the realm . . .' continued Miranda.

'Get him in the chair. Get Anthony effing Hopkins in the chair now!' I said, like an angry alpha female whose taxi has taken her on a route she doesn't care for.

'National treasure,' Miranda was ad-libbing wildly. 'Oscar-honoured, flesh-eating . . .'

The floor manager was rushing Anthony Hopkins into the chair, the soundman miking him up as they went.

'National treasure I cannot stress enough times, actor, time-honoured, Sir Anthony . . .'

It wasn't Anthony Hopkins.

'Hopkins! Sir Anthony!' Miranda said, brightly, even though it clearly wasn't. 'Has Hannibal Lecter dogged you throughout your career?'

'Actually, I'm here to talk about the possible gay gene in the womb environment,' said the man, as Sir Anthony

Hopkins loomed up behind Miranda, doing his Hannibal Lecter flesh-eating face.

Afterwards, just as Miranda flopped down next to me in the control room, saying, 'Jesus, who do you have to screw to get a mojito round here?' Richard Finch threw open the door, gave one of his looks and said, 'Bridget! Miranda! This is Peri Campos, our new network controller.' He gestured to a high-heeled woman behind him. 'And these are the systems analysis team who have been observing our show today.' A group of people shuffled into the small control room.

'As they will for the next four weeks, looking for where our staffing cuts can most effectively be made,' finished Peri Campos, who was very young, wearing some sort of designer bondage outfit, and surrounded by youths sporting beards and man-buns. 'Pruning,' she continued. 'I love that word. It kind of brings a rush of blood to my teeth.'

7 p.m. *Sit Up Britain* **loos.** I am going to be fired and replaced by young people in man-buns.

7.03 p.m. It was my last sexual experience ever. It was a pity shag.

7.04 p.m. I am like those teachers we had at school who were just permanently single and wore thick white powder and red lipstick and were called 'Miss' something or other and seemed like ancient alien creatures. Now I have become just like them and— Oh, goody! Telephone!

*

7.10 p.m. Was Tom. 'So what time you coming to this Archer-Biro Prize thing.'

Mind started whirring.

'Bridget? BRIDGET?'

'I cannot go,' I said in an eerie, sepulchral voice. 'To the Archer-Biro Prize.'

'Oh, for fuck's sakes, darling. You can't still be maundering on about Mark Darcy. You're a radiant superpower sex goddess, and he's an uptight serial-bigamist bore with a poker up his arse. We'll see you in the Sky Bar at 7.30. Get your freak on, bitch.'

8 p.m. Bankside Ballroom, South London. As we hurried up the stairs into the event, Shazzer was in full fuckwittage auto-rant.

'Bastaaaaaaaaards!'

There was a brief altercation with the black-clad twenty-somethings controlling the list. Shazzer had to explain that there was no question of Tom being excluded for not being on the list, it was clearly Archer-Biro HOMOPHOBIA, which would NOT play out well on social media, etc., etc.

The twenty-somethings, terrified, waved us through, and Shazzer continued her rant as we took on the next set of stairs.

'How dare he shag you at a christening and then just DISAPPEAR? He's an emotionally constipated, wanton, drunken . . .'

'Insecurely attached,' added Tom, who is now (try not to laugh) a psychotherapist.

'Self-righteous fuckwitted bastard!' continued Shazzer loudly, as we burst into the room to find Le Tout Literary London gathered, holding their wine and little plastic cups full of unidentifiable food. The nominee authoresses, from a wide range of nations, were lined up on the stage: here a batik headdress, there a Guatemalan robe, there a full burka.

'Shhh!' The back row of literati turned around, appalled, as the chairwoman, dressed in an Oscar-like glittering gown, took the microphone.

'Ladies and – not to be forgotten – gentlemen!'

She paused for a – frankly faint – ripple of amusement. 'Welcome to the Archer-Biro Prize for Women's Fiction: now in its fifteenth glorious year. The Archer-Biro Prize was conceived broadly, but quintessentially, for the eradication of "chick lit".'

'I'm just too old,' I muttered.

'For the promotion of the serious, empowered . . .'

I leaned in to Shazzer. 'No one will ever sleep with me again, ever, ever, ever.'

'. . . the valid, strong . . .'

'Last ever sexual experience my arse,' Shazzer said.

'. . . the intuitive, female imperative . . .'

'We'll have you laid before the night's out,' said Miranda.

'Will you girls be QUIET,' hissed Jung Chang, who was hogging the bar.

'Fuck, sorry,' I muttered, then felt a hand brush across my bum. I froze, then looked round to see the retreating back of a familiar figure making his way through the crowd.

'And now, to present the award, I'd like to welcome TV personality, former chairman of Pergamon Press, and – a little bird tells me – nascent NOVELIST! Daniel Cleaver!'

Gaaaaaaaah!

'What's he doing here?' said Tom. 'I thought he was in Transylvania with Princess Disney of Bimboland.'

'Ladies and gentlemen, Archer-Biro,' Daniel began, looking toned and glowing, like a successful politician who's just had a facial. 'It is a tremendously arousing honour to be standing amongst such an array of radiant lady finalists: almost like wandering into the Alternative Miss World Competition.'

I flinched on his behalf, waiting for roars of outrage, but instead there was a ripple of amusement.

'Oh, isn't he a hoot?' said Pat Barker, turning and wrinkling her nose amusedly.

'I'm actually just waiting for the swimwear segment,' Daniel continued.

There were roars of laughter.

'Obviously, it has taken me rather longer to learn to pronounce our esteemed finalists' names than to read their actual works of rare genius. The result, which I hold in this gilded Ryman's envelope, was, apparently, an extremely close shave – something, of course, never to be undertaken by the ladies assembled before me.'

The strong, female literary voices were now beside themselves with mirth.

'And now, with trembling hands, and with thanks to Trinity College, Cambridge, for a perfunctory grounding in Proto-Indo European, I pronounce the winner to be . . .'

He opened the envelope with a huge amount of fuss. 'Yes, it's like trying to extract a condom from its packaging, and actually— Oh! My darlings! My dearest readers and finalists! It's a draw! – between Omaguli Qulawe for *The Sound of Timeless Tears* and Angela Binks for *The Soundless Tears of Time*.'

As soon as the speeches were over, Daniel was swamped by a sea of gorgeous young publicists and I dived off to the Ladies to recover my composure.

'Don't even start with that line of thought,' said Tom, as I excused myself from the table. 'Give it a few more years and all the power is with the women. Fuckwittage becomes a luxury you can't afford when your hair's falling out and your stomach's hanging over your waistband.'

Had total meltdown in the Ladies, thinking that I looked a hundred years old, and started plastering myself with make-up, at which Tom put his head round the door and said, 'Stop right there, darling, or you'll come out looking like Barbara Cartland.' Eventually I emerged from the Ladies into the hall and came face-to-face with Daniel.

'Jones, you gorgeous creature,' he cried, delighted. 'You look younger and more attractive than when I last saw you five years ago. No, seriously, Jones, I don't know whether to marry you or adopt you.'

'Daniel!' said Julian Barnes, approaching with his thin-lipped smile.

'Julian! Have you met my young niece, Bridget Jones?'

9 p.m. In loos again, touching up own youthful beauty with more blusher. Blurry good party. Thing about Daniel is he really is very charming and I really don't feel old any more.

Which was, in a way, what I *think* the entire Archer-Biro Prize was saying one ought *not* to allow oneself to feel because of a man.

'Go for it, girl,' said Tom, handing me a drink as I emerged from the loos again. 'Get back on that horse.'

10 p.m. Daniel and I were stumbling, wine-filled, in the flow of drunken attendees pouring out of the venue.

'So what happened to the princess?' I said.

'Oh, over, over. Shame, really. I think I would ultimately have made rather an effective king: cruel, but beloved.'

'Oh dear. What went wrong?'

'Perfection blunted the horn, Jones. Every night, the same glossy hair splayed on the pillow. The same exquisite features frozen in ecstasy. It was as if the very sexual act had been digitally performance-captured. You, Jones, in contrast, are like that mysterious, lumpy parcel that arrives on a Christmas morning, odd, a little misshapen but . . .'

'. . . one you always want to get inside. Well, thank you, Daniel. Lovely to catch up! I'll be getting a cab now.'

'I meant it as a compliment, Jones. Besides, firstly, there are no cabs; and, secondly, if there were, you would be competing for them with five hundred other giants of the literary stage, all of them with full beards and moustaches.'

I was trying to call a minicab, but the voicemail was saying, 'All our customer service agents are currently busy, as we are currently experiencing unusually long wait times for this location.'

'Look,' said Daniel, 'my flat is three minutes away. Let me arrange you a ride home from there. Least I can do.'

I watched as Annie Proulx and Pat Barker snapped up the last remaining cab, Jung Chang bounding in behind them.

10.30 p.m. Daniel's flat. I stood in Daniel's familiar, designer shag-pad, overlooking the Thames. All the car companies were still 'currently experiencing unexpected delays'.

'Seen Darcy since he returned?' said Daniel, holding out a glass of champagne. 'In emotional ignominy and failure? Hardly surprising for a man who looks in the mirror every morning and is startled by a complete stranger. Did he weep after sex? Or before? Or was it during? I forget.'

'Right, Daniel, that's enough,' I said indignantly. 'I have not come into your flat to be treated to a litany of very unpositive bad karmic vibes about somebody who – '

Suddenly Daniel kissed me on the lips. Oh God, he was such a great kisser.

'No, no, we mustn't,' I said weakly.

'Yes, yes, we must. You know the one thing people most regret when they're about to die? Not that they didn't save the world, or rise to the pinnacle of their career, but that they didn't have more sex.'

TUESDAY 27 JUNE

8 p.m. My flat. Staring psychopathically at phone. Still no word from either of them. Is this going to go on for the rest of my life? Am I going to be getting drunk on sherry with Mark and Daniel over dominoes in the old people's home, then getting furious because they've shagged me and haven't asked me to play Scrabble?

8.05 p.m. Cannot believe I am still behaving like this after sex after all these years – as if I have sat an exam and am waiting for my results. Am going to call Shazzer.

8.15 p.m. 'Doesn't count with exes,' decreed Shaz.

'That's exactly what Miranda said! Why?'

'Because you've already fucked up the relationship.'

'So I already know I've failed?'

8.30 p.m. I am going to give up men. I eschew them.

Four

Perimenopause

Three Months Later

10 p.m. My flat. Everything is terrible. I mean, I just can't believe that this is— Oh, goody! Doorbell!

11 p.m. Was Shazzer, Tom and Miranda, bursting into the flat, completely plastered.

'Darling! You're alive!' said Tom.

'What's going the fuck on?' enquired Shaz.

'What do you mean?'

'You haven't answered calls, texts, emails, anything all weekend. You're in total techno-purdah.'

'What is she googling?'

I leapt at the laptop and wrestled it from their hands.

'Perimenopause! She's been googling perimenopause for seven hours. She's *signed up* to hotflush.com.'

'For some women perimenopause can begin as early as thirty-five,' I gabbled. 'In years to come all women will automatically freeze their eggs, build their careers, microwave them, and Bob's your uncle, but . . .'

'Why do you think you're perimenopausal?'

I stared at them, embarrassed.

'Have your periods become irregular?' said Shazzer.

I nodded, almost in tears. 'Gone, and I'm getting

49

middle-age spread. Look, I've had to buy jeans a size bigger.'

I showed them my stomach. But instead of looking sympathetic they started exchanging glances.

'Er, Bridget,' began Tom. 'Just, um, a thought. Perhaps a random thought, but . . .'

'You have done a fucking pregnancy test, right?' said Shazzer.

I reeled. How could she be so cruel?

'I told you – I'm barren,' I said. 'I can't be pregnant because I'm perimenopausal, so I can't have children anymore.'

Miranda looked as though she was trying not to laugh. 'You know, the whole "doesn't count with exes thing" in the summer? Mark and Daniel? Did you use condoms?'

This was unbearable.

'Yes!' I said, starting to feel quite cross now. 'Of course I used condoms.' I picked up my handbag and held out the packet. 'These condoms.'

The packet was passed between them as if it was a piece of evidence from *CSI: Miami*.

'Bridget,' said Shazzer. 'These are eco-dolphin-friendly condoms and they're two years out of date.'

'Well, so?' I said. 'I mean, sell-by dates are just there to sell more products, aren't they? They're not real.'

'The whole point of the dolphin-friendliness is that they dissolve over time,' said Miranda.

'Look,' said Shazzer, standing up and putting on her coat, 'never fucking mind the fucking dolphins. Let's get the fuck to the late-night chemist.'

*

As we drove through the streets to the late-night chemist I felt like I was driving through the graveyard of my fertile years – there the tree where Daniel threw my knickers after the Pergamon Press Christmas party, there the corner where Mark and I had our first kiss in the snow, there the doorstep where Mark Darcy first said, 'I love you, just as you are.'

Back in the flat, Shazzer was banging on the bathroom door.

'It takes two minutes, OK?' I said.

'What if she's pregnant with both of them? Like twins?' I heard Tom whisper loudly.

'You can't,' hissed Miranda drunkenly. 'The first sperm blocks the second, or something.'

'What about when someone has one black twin and one white twin?'

'That's different eggs but the same sperm.'

This was not how I had imagined this moment would be. I thought I would be with the square-jawed love of my life in a renovated farmhouse in the Cotswolds with poured concrete floors and shaggy rugs, possibly interior-designed by Jade Jagger.

'This is just completely ridiculous. A woman can't have black eggs and white eggs,' growled Shazzer.

'Speckled eggs?' suggested Tom, as I emerged from the bathroom.

'Look, she's got the stick.'

'Give me that.'

Shazzer and Tom both lunged at the stick, knocking it out of my hands. We watched as it twirled up into the air and landed gently on the carpet, then stared at it in awed wonder. There was an unmistakable blue line across the little window.

'You can't be . . .'

'. . . a little bit pregnant,' finished Tom.

'*A. May. Zing,*' said Miranda.

I couldn't believe it.

In the background I could hear the friends continuing:

'But she's been drinking and smoking.'

'Oh my God, you're right – she's killed the baby.'

'The baby's dead.'

'And she doesn't know who the father is.'

'What are we going to do?'

But none of it mattered at all. I felt like trumpets were tooting and harps were tinkling. Clouds were parting, the sun's rays bursting through, while little birds tweeted with joy. I was having a baby.

FIVE

WHODUNNIT?

9 a.m. Obstetrician's office, London. 'So, which of the times do you think I would have got pregnant on?' I said, hopefully.

'Does it matter?' said Dr Rawlings, a stern woman with a crisp, humourless manner.

'Yes! Such a special moment! We want to know which one it is so we can treasure it.'

'Well, you can't. You'll have to treasure both of them.'

'But surely one date is more likely than the other?'

'Actually, one's a bit early, and the other's a bit late. Are you sure there wasn't another "treasurable occasion" in between?'

'Quite sure, thank you,' I said, primly. 'So, of the two, which one would you go for?'

'No idea: both equally likely.'

'Have a guess.'

'No.'

'Just pretend you're putting money on a horse.'

'No.'

'What about the scan?'

'Ten to thirteen weeks: you're thirteen.'

'Will that show when the conception was?'

'No. Now call this number to fix a date for the scan,' she said, getting up. 'And you'll be able to bring the daddy with you, won't you?'

Distinctly heard her adding, under her breath, 'If you can work out which one he is.'

'Just out of interest . . .' I burst out, suddenly.

'Yeeees?'

'If someone did have an element of confusion about who the father was . . .'

'You need to get samples from them – blood, hair, fingernails, teeth.'

'Teeth?'

'No, not teeth, Bridget,' she said wearily. 'Hair, fingernails, blood, saliva – all better than teeth.'

'And if someone wanted to get the DNA from the baby?'

'You need an amniocentesis. Which is probably a good idea, anyway, when you're a geriatric mother.'

'GERIATRIC MOTHER?'

'Yes. Over the age of thirty-six you are, technically, a geriatric mother.'

THURSDAY 5 OCTOBER

'Look on the bright side,' Tom was saying, as he, Shaz and Magda walked me to the amniocentesis. 'You'll be able to claim your pension and child support at the same time.'

'This is just so stressful!' Magda was hyperventilating. 'Bridget, you can't have a baby without a father. One father.'

'No, honestly, Magda, it'll be absolutely fine,' I said, suddenly retching.

'Darling, anything we can do to help?' said Tom.

'Thanks, Tom. Could you get me a baked potato? Oh, and a chocolate croissant and some bacon. I'm scared; I don't want a great big needle inside me.'

'Look, the whole thing's completely unnecessary anyway,' said Shaz. 'If it starts dragging you towards every attractive woman you pass, you'll know it's Daniel's. And if it feels like it's got a poker up its arse, it's Mark Darcy's.'

7 p.m. My flat. Just returned from heaven/narrowly averted amnio nightmare.

'So, the baby's OK?' I said, as Dr Rawlings slithered the ultrasound over my stomach.

'Sound as a bell. Don't worry, you're not the first woman not to realise she's pregnant and spend the first few months still having little drinkies. Here, you take a look at that.'

She turned the screen towards me and that was it. It was love. She was all blurry – with a little round head, like, like . . . a baby. A miniature person inside me! A nose, a mouth, little fists up near her mouth! – the most beautiful thing I'd ever seen.

'Right!' said Dr Rawlings. She turned round holding a giant needle. It was insane. It was about a foot long. 'Now, I do have to tell you, there are certain risks of miscarriage with amniocentesis, particularly at your age, but these have to be weighed against—'

'Get away from me!' I yelled, jumping up from the table. 'What are you DOING? Are you out of your mind? You'll MURDER my baby! You'll skewer her like Hamlet from behind the arras.'

Found myself, to my alarm, holding my stomach tenderly like one of the Smug Mothers at the christening.

'Do you want to feel my bump?' I said.

'I just did, Bridget. That's how we just saw the nice picture of the lovely baby, remember? Now, are we going to get on with this?'

'No, no, it's fine,' I gabbled, gathering my stuff. 'No risks, no DNA. Just don't come near my baby with that needle.'

SATURDAY 7 OCTOBER

Calories 4,824. (But am pregnant, right? So world of food is my oyster. Though not oysters, obviously, as toxic to baby.) Toasted bagels: 3. (Potassium, or fibre?) Cheese 8 oz. (Protein.) (But not goat's cheese – soft cheese toxic to baby.) Broccoli: 3 florets. (Excellent Crossover Food, but doesn't count, as threw up after – baby hates broccoli.) Cheesy potatoes: 3. (Baby loves cheesy potatoes, and unborn babies have an instinctive knowledge of what they *need*.)

4 p.m. Just back from baby shopping. Have bought completely adorable peach playsuit with a floral bandana from ILoveGorgeous and laid it out on the bed, for all the world like it is a little baby girl. Almost wonder if could purchase doll baby to dress it up in to practise, but would that be creepy? Am so excited but at the same time find self feeling strangely lazy, sleepy and distracted, almost as if am a bit stoned. Must make sure no one finds out about this at work just yet. Also probably not tell Mum just yet. Also am definitely going to really mentally address the issue of the father. Definitely.

But will just take a minute to relish how lovely it is. I'm going to have a baby!

SIX

TELLING THE TRUTH

Noon. The Electric Bar, Portobello Road. 'You do have to tell them, Bridge,' said Miranda.

I nodded, sucking diet tonic through a straw. Even though we were sitting in the Electric, my urge to drink alcohol had suddenly disappeared. The very thought of it made me feel strangely acidic and queasy almost as if I had a hangover, which is odd when you think about it.

'Bridget!'

'What?' I said, jumping.

'You have to tell them: the fathers.'

'Oh yes, no, I do,' I said. 'I will. Shall we get some more chips? Do you want to feel my bump?'

They all somewhat wearily and perfunctorily patted my bump.

'Start with Daniel,' said Tom. 'To practise.'

'Text him now,' said Miranda.

'She can't just text him out of the blue.'

'Yes, I can. I can do what I like. I've got a baby to look after.'

I picked up the phone, bold as you please, and texted:

```
Cleaver, Jones here. I want to talk to
you. Can I see you this week?
```

He texted back immediately:

```
DANIEL CLEAVER
Rather out of the blue, Jones, but why the
hell not? Be delighted to see you. Friday
night? I shall pick you up and take you
out to dinner in my new car.
```

Blimey. Is it that easy? Have I been sitting here being so obsessed with making sure people think I don't fancy them, in case they think I'm needy, that they actually think I don't fancy them?

FRIDAY 13 OCTOBER

7 p.m. Daniel's car, South London. 'Like the car, do you, Jones?'

As Daniel and I zoomed across Waterloo Bridge, I was desperately trying to find a moment to bring up the baby before we got to the restaurant, lest the whole thing caused a public scene, but Daniel was completely obsessed with his new Mercedes.

'It seems like it's purring like a kitten, but put your foot down and whooomph!'

Daniel suddenly accelerated, causing an alarming lurch in my stomach.

'Do you like the pale grey interiors, Jones? I was going to go for black, or even a rather luscious blood red, but I thought this was delicate and actually rather pretty.'

*

Daniel had chosen Nobu restaurant on Park Lane, which was the sort of place where one might easily run into Posh and Becks or indeed Brad and Angelina (in which case I could have settled the argument once and for all with Mum about whether or not Maddox was how Angelina 'got' Brad Pitt).

Sadly, there were no visible celebrities. It was rather, I assume, like going on safari and finding there were no lions or tigers. There was, however, an unmistakable scent of fish in the air.

As the waiter led us to the table, Daniel still hadn't paused for breath long enough for me to bring up, well, anything, really. He had now moved on from his new car to his new novel, *The Poetics of Time*.

'Conceptually, it's *Time's Arrow* in reverse. The characters believe time is moving backwards, but it's actually moving forwards.'

'But wouldn't that just mean time is moving in the direction it normally does move in?' I said.

'It's a conceptual novel, Jones. It's existential.'

What was the matter with him? Normally Daniel's only interest was getting you to tell him what knickers you used to wear at school.

'Yes, but still,' I said doggedly, as the waiters brought us the menus, 'wouldn't it be a bit obvious, that it wasn't?'

The menu was all fish, different kinds of fish: sushi fish, tempura fish, fish that had been spoon-fed on sake for hundreds of years. I felt the baby thrashing in a frenzy of fish outrage.

'Wasn't what, Jones?'

'Going backwards. I mean, if time was going backwards, you'd notice straight away. Cars would be going backwards. Fish would be swimming backwards,' I said, feeling a lurch in my stomach.

'Fish?'

Through my new, pregnancy-induced passivity, I let Daniel order the food and carry on about his backwards-though-not-backwards book. It was all very odd. Daniel seemed to have developed some sort of urge to be taken seriously. Maybe it was to do with the advancing years. The car too! I was having a baby and Daniel was having a cliché.

'You see, this is an alternate conceptual universe, Jones,' continued Daniel. 'There are no fish in *The Poetics of Time*.'

'Well! That's something to be grateful for!' I said, brightly. As the waiter placed the food – all fish – in front of us, I felt I really had to get away from *The Poetics of Time* and on to the meat of the matter.

'It's a new reality which makes one question one's very—'

'Right, right, it sounds very . . . Look, Daniel, there's something I need to—'

'I know, I know, I know, I know,' he said, and paused for dramatic effect. Then he switched into the more typical Daniel seducer mode, leaning towards me and looking deep into my eyes, with an air of flimsy sincerity.

'I was appalling, Jones. There should have been phone calls, sobbing gratitude for our explosive night. There should have been floral tributes, trinkets, chocolates, delicately embossed with our two names, entwined on little hearts. But I've been in *total* writing lockdown hell: editing, galleys, the launch. You can't imagine the creative weight of having an entire novel in one's head and . . .'

'Excuse me.'

'Yes, Jones?'

'Could you shut up? You're talking bollox.'

'Ah, you're right, Jones. Right as ever. Remind me what knickers you wore at school?'

I suddenly retched.

'Everything all right?'

'I'm not sure I can manage the fish. Do you think I could order a baked potato?'

'Ah, well, the thing is, you see, Nobu, being a Japanese restaurant, does not make a forte out of baked potatoes, jam roly-poly, pork pies, that sort of thing. You've just ordered a lovely Pink Miso Trout, which has been marinated in seaweed and fed on sake for four hundred years. Eat it up, there's a good girl.'

I had to concentrate so hard on keeping the food down that by the time the doorman was handing me back into Daniel's new car, with its new-leather smell, I still hadn't brought up the fact that the baby, who was now wrestling furiously with a Miso Trout inside me, was even there.

'Lovely evening,' murmured Daniel, clicking something on the dashboard and revving the car with a roar.

'Daniel, there's something I have to . . .'

The Miso Trout was suddenly rushing upwards towards my throat.

'Dnl stp the crr,' I tried to say, putting my hand over my mouth as it filled with sick.

'Didn't quite catch that, Jones.'

But it was too late.

'Christ alive, Jones, what's going on? This is a nightmare. This is hell. Are you the Exorcist?' a melting-down Daniel cried, as sick spurted out from behind my hand all over his pale grey interior.

11 p.m. My flat. Little sweetheart, I'm so sorry about all this. I'll make it up to you, I promise. You just stay safe in there and leave it all to me. I'm going to show you the best time . . . I think I'd better call your grandad.

SATURDAY 14 OCTOBER

Dad's club, London. It was so lovely to see Dad. I told him everything and he just looked at me with those kind, wise eyes and gave me a big hug. We were sitting in the library. There were old books, maps, globes; a sooty coal fire, and leather armchairs whose tattiness went so far beyond the distressed as to be practically psychotic.

'I feel like a crack whore, or one of those women on *Jerry Springer* who's slept with her own grandson,' I said. 'Do you want to feel my bump?'

'We're all just an impulse away from *The Jerry Springer Show*, love,' said Dad, patting his embryonic granddaughter affectionately. 'I'm not even sure myself if you belong to me or that young curate who did a stint at the vicarage forty years ago.'

I gasped.

'I'm joking, pet. But you haven't done anything that ninety per cent of people in the world wouldn't have done in your position.'

We both looked round at the aged gentlemen club members, most of whom were dozing quietly in their armchairs.

'Eighty-five per cent?' said Dad. 'Look, pet. You never go too far wrong by just telling the truth.'

'You mean tell Mum?' I said, horrified.

'Well, no, maybe not your mum just yet. But with Mark and Daniel, just tell the truth and see where it takes you.'

SUNDAY 15 OCTOBER

2 p.m. My flat. Sitting on the floor, hands trembling, I dialled Daniel's number, feeling the six collective eyes of Tom, Miranda and Shazzer boring into me.

'Yeees, Jones?' said Daniel into the phone. 'Is my ear about to be sprayed with—'

'Daniel, I'm sixteen weeks pregnant,' I blurted.

The line went dead.

'He hung up on me!'

'Fuckwit, total, total fucking fuckwit from hell with a tail.'

'How can any human fuckwit do that?' I said, fuming. 'That's it. I'm through with bloody men. They're irresponsible; self-indulgent . . . Does anyone want to feel my bump?'

'You have to find some way of externalising these angry thoughts and feelings,' said Tom in his creepy therapist's voice and patting the bump nervously, as if the baby was going to jump out and be sick on him. 'Perhaps by writing them down and burning them?'

'OK,' I said, marching over to the kitchen table and grabbing a Post-it pad and a box of matches.

'No!' yelled Shazzer. 'No fires! Use the phone.'

'Okeedokeee.'

I typed into the phone. 'Daniel, you are a selfish, shallow—'

'Give it to me, give it to me,' slurred Shazzer, grabbing the phone. She typed 'fuckwitted, crap writer' and then pressed send.

'We were supposed to BURN IT,' I said in horror.

'What? The phone?'

'She was supposed to express the angry thoughts and feelings, then send them into the universe,' said Tom. 'Not text them to the object of the angry thoughts and . . . Here, have we run out of wine?'

'Oh, God. And he might be the father of my unborn child.'

'Iss fine,' said Tom, in a drunk yet soothing voice. 'Do him good to hear it.'

'Tom, shut up. Bridget, you've done your practising. Now text Mark,' said Miranda.

*

So I did. I simply texted: 'I would like to see you.' And, to my utter astonishment, he wanted to meet me immediately.

SUNDAY 15 OCTOBER

I stood on the doorstep of Mark's tall white-stuccoed house in Holland Park, as I'd stood before, before so many earth-shattering events, sad, happy, sexual, emotional, triumphant, disastrous, dramatic. The light was on upstairs in his office: he was working as usual. What would he say? Would he reject me as a drunken slag? Might he be pleased? But then . . .

'Bridget!' said the intercom. 'Are you actually still there or have you rung the doorbell and run away?'

'I'm here,' I said.

The door opened a few seconds later. Mark was in sexy work mode: suit trousers, shirt a little undone, sleeves rolled up and the familiar watch on his wrist.

'Come in,' he said. I followed him into the kitchen. It was exactly the same: spotless, streamlined cabinets where you couldn't tell which was the dishwasher, which was the cereal cupboard and which was the pig bin.

'So!' said Mark, stiffly. 'How's life treating you? Work good?'

'Yes. How's yours? Work, I mean.'

'Oh, good, well, shit actually.'

He gave that conspiratorial half-smile I so loved.

71

'Trying and failing to extract Hanza Farzad from the clutches of the king of Kutar.'

'Ah.'

I gazed out at the garden and trees, the leaves beginning to turn, mind racing. I mean my mind, not the trees' minds. Trees do not have minds: unless you're the mind of Prince Charles, or perhaps in Daniel Cleaver's novel. Our whole future rested on these next few babies, I mean moments. I started to rerehearse what I was going to say. It had to be subtle, slowly built up to.

'All caught up with international trade, of course,' Mark was going on. 'Always the problem with the Middle East: endless layers of subterfuge, deceit, conflicted interest . . .'

'Excuse me.'

'Yes?'

There was a pause. 'The garden looks lovely,' I eventually said.

'Thank you. Of course, it's a devil to keep up with the leaves.'

'Yes it must be.'

'Yes.'

'Yup . . . Mark?'

'Yes, Bridget?'

Oh God, oh God. I just couldn't do it. I wanted to savour these last few moments when everything seemed like it used to be.

'Is that a conker tree?'

'Yes. It is a conker tree and that one's a magnolia and . . .'

'Oh, and what is that one?'

'Bridget!'

'I'm pregnant.'

Mark's face was a mess of emotions.

'How much, how long, pregnant?'

'Sixteen weeks.'

'The christening?'

'Do you want to feel my bump?'

'Yes.' He put his hand on it briefly, then said, 'Excuse me.'

He left the room. I could hear him going upstairs. What was he going to do? Come down with lawsuit papers?

The door burst open.

'This is the single most wonderful piece of information I have ever been given in my entire life.'

He came over and took me in his arms, and the familiar scent of him, the reassuring feel of him, washed over me.

'It's . . . I feel almost as if clouds are dispersing.'

He held me away from him, looking at me with tenderness in his brown eyes.

'When one's own childhood has been . . . when one has somehow . . . I never found it possible to believe that love could translate into a home life. That one could create a home we could bring a child into, that was somehow different' – he looked like a small boy – 'different from one's own.'

I hugged him, this time, and stroked his hair.

'And now,' he said, coming out of the embrace, with that rare smile he has, 'in a moment of . . . *unadulterated* passion, the decision has been made for us. And I'm the happiest man alive.'

There was a knock on the door and Fatima, Mark's long-time housekeeper, appeared. 'Oh!' she beamed. 'Mees Jones! You back? Mr Darcy, your car is here.'

'Oh my goodness. I completely forgot. I have a Law Society dinner . . .'

'No, Mark, it's fine, you already said you had a dinner.'

'But my car can . . . we can drop you off.'

'I've got my new car, that's fine.'

'Tomorrow, we'll meet tomorrow night?'

'Yes.'

7 p.m. My flat. This is unbearable. I'm pregnant, and Mark wants the baby and if I hadn't slept with Daniel as well this would be a complete fairy tale and we would all be so happy but . . . Oh God. Mark and I did occasionally take chances, so maybe sleeping with Daniel is *why* I'm pregnant.

Bloody dolphin condoms. But then I wouldn't have been having the baby, if I hadn't tried to save the dolphins from swallowing undissolved condoms. So actually I should be grateful to the condoms, if only the already-dolphin-friendly baby could tell me whose dolphin-friendly baby she is.

It's all my fault. But Daniel is so funny and charming.

It's like they're two halves of the perfect man, who'll spend the rest of their lives each wanting to outdo the other one. And now it's all enacting itself in my stomach.

7.15 p.m. Toilet really is wonderful invention. Is just amazing to have such an item in one's home, which can so calmly, cleanly and efficiently take all the sick away. Love the lovely toilet. Is cool and solid, calm and dependable. Is fine just to lie here and keep it handy. Maybe it is not Mark I really love but the toilet. Oh, goody, telephone! Maybe Mark asking how I am! Maybe I will just tell him the whole story and he'll forgive me.

8 p.m. Was Tom: 'Bridget, am I a horrible person?'

'Tom! No! You're a lovely person!'

Source of Horrible Person neurosis was that Tom had seen an 'acquaintance' (i.e., guy he shagged once), Jesus, at the front of the gym snack-bar queue, gone up to say hi, and then asked Jesus to order him a wheatgrass smoothie.

'The thing is,' Tom obsessed, 'the thought of queue-jumping had – I think – crossed my mind before I decided to say hello to Jesus. So I'm one of those people who coldly, cynically, tries to make things better for themselves at the expense of others: like avoiding buying a round in the pub by going to the toilet.'

'But the key issue you're missing, Tom,' I said – happy to escape from my own fucked-up situation for a moment, whilst simultaneously feeling a nagging certainty that sooner or later Tom was going to remember about my fucked-up situation then decide he was a horrible person anyway for forgetting to ask about it – 'is that, actually, saying hello to a friend is a nice thing, and joining Jesus

75

for a gym-time beverage is much more friendly than just abandoning him and going to the back of the queue.'

'But then I did abandon Jesus and went and drank the wheatgrass smoothie with Eduardo because he's hotter. You see, I am a horrible person, aren't I?'

Mind was busily trying to turn the minuscule social gay gaffe into a random act of kindness, but then Tom crashed in with: 'OK. I get it. I am a horrible person. Goodbye.'

The phone rang again.

'Oh, hello, darling, I was just ringing to see what you wanted for Christmas?' – my mother. Flirted briefly with throwing the cat amongst the pigeons by asking for a Bugaboo stroller, but knew she had really called to talk about something else. 'Bridget, will you come to the Queen's visit rehearsal on the twenty-eighth? Mavis is making a huge thing about family values and, as well as making *constant* little digs about me not having grand-children, she's trying to make out that I haven't done as much for the village as her over the years, but I have, darling, haven't I?'

'Of course you have, Mum. Think of all the food! The gherkins!' I encouraged, starting to gag. 'The Scotch eggs! The raspberry pavlovas!'

'Yes! The Salmon à la King! All those salmons!'

Gaah! 'You've been a bastion of village life, Mum,' I said. 'You go sock it to that Mavis!'

('Sock it to'? Where did that come from?)

'Thank you, darling. Ooh, must whizz! I've left gammon and pineapple in.'

Was just recovering from the latest vomit, embracing the beloved toilet, when the phone rang again.

Was Tom: 'I forgot to ask you how it went with Mark. You see? Horrible person. Don't deserve to talk to you. Goodbye.'

Looked confusedly at the phone for a minute, then, thinking about the baby, decided to microwave a cheesy potato.

9 p.m. There you go, little sweetheart: cheesy potato.

We have to tell the truth, don't we? That's one of the things we're always going to do. Even if it means being very, very brave. Even if we really don't want to.

MONDAY 16 OCTOBER

Mark's whole house was turned into a baby-welcoming committee, with flowers, baby supplies and a banner across the kitchen saying CONGRATULATIONS BRIDGET.

Fatima was bustling about, beaming. She hugged me and then left the room with her usual discretion.

'You mustn't carry anything,' said Mark, taking my handbag. 'Sit here and put your feet up.'

He sat me on a bar stool at the kitchen counter and tried to lift my feet up onto another bar stool. We both laughed.

'Look what I brought down from the attic for him. I used to love this. Look!'

An old Scalextric car set was laid out in the – I supposed

you could now call it – family room, where the comfy sofas and chairs were.

I was laughing and fighting back tears. 'She might not be ready for that STRAIGHT away, but . . .'

Mark bounded over to the fridge. 'Look what I've got in here!'

There were two packs of Huggies nappies.

'I thought that was where you were supposed to keep them: so they're nice and cool on the little bottom. No? I'm practising. You'll move in here, of course? The three of us? It's as if we've been given a second chance! A second chance at life!'

My dad's words were repeating themselves in my ear. 'You never go too far wrong by just telling the truth.'

'Mark.'

He stopped in his tracks at my tone.

'What? Bridget, what's wrong? The baby? Is there something wrong?'

'No, no. The baby's fine.'

'Oh, thank God.'

'It's just . . . there is one tiny complication.'

'Right, right. We can deal with anything. What is it?'

'It's just, I was so upset after the christening when you said you didn't want to get back together and use up any more of my fertile years . . .'

'I'm so very sorry. Believe me, I've been wretched about it, and torn as to whether I should contact you. I allowed myself to be swayed by Jeremy. He caught me in the hall-way of the hotel, when I went out for breakfast, and said it was very wrong of me to be messing around with you at this point in your life unless I was absolutely certain that I could be constant and be a husband to you. At that point, so raw from the divorce, I didn't feel that, morally, responsibly, I should . . .'

I closed my eyes. Why couldn't I learn not to be so insecure, not to flee at the first hint of rejection? To understand that there might be more to it than me being too old or too fat or silly?

'I felt inadequate,' he said, 'unequal to the task, but now . . .'

'It's just I was so hurt.'

'I am so very sorry, Bridget.'

'I just felt so old, you see, that I . . .'

'But no, *I* felt so old. What did you do?'

'Is that an elm tree?'

'Bridget.'

'I slept with Daniel Cleaver.'

'The same DAY?'

'No, no: a few days later. I felt as if my sexual days were over, and he was saying I looked so young he didn't know whether to marry me or adopt me, and the friends were saying "Get back on that horse" and . . .'

'You used protection with, with . . . both parties?'

Mark was opening and closing the stainless-steel cabinets.

'Yes, but they were . . . eco-condoms. It turned out they were past their sell-by date and they dissolve because of the dolphins.'

He opened another immaculate stainless-steel door and a huge pile of mess fell out – papers, photographs, old shirts, pencils, leaflets. He tried to stuff it all back in. He shut the door on it firmly. I saw his shoulders stiffen and he turned back to me.

'Yes, no, I can quite see how all that would happen. There's no necessity to explain.'

He opened another cupboard, found a bottle of Scotch and started pouring himself a glass.

'Can you find out? I mean technically the paternity, who the . . . the . . . father is?' he said, gulping down the Scotch.

'Not without risking the baby.'

'But surely . . .'

'I know. But I'm not going to risk it. Giant needle thing. Horrible.'

He started pacing, in his agitated way. 'Right, right, of course. I see now. That would explain why, when we did take the occasional chance . . .'

Then he turned to me: composed, steely.

'I expect you'll be wanting to get an early night.'

'Mark. Don't. She could be our baby. There's a fifty per cent chance, at least.'

'It's kind of you to say.'

'It just takes a moment, an impulse, one bad decision.'

'Yes, I know. I see it every day of my professional life: tragic. Life turns on a sixpence. But I don't want that in my personal life, I'm afraid.'

'I'm so, so sorry.'

'It's life. One must play with the cards one is dealt. Jolly good.'

There was nothing to be done with him in this state. He walked me in silence back to the car and I cried all the way home.

SEVEN

FUCKWITTAGE

8 p.m. My flat. 'That's it, I'm an idiot. It's all my fault. He'll never forgive me.'

'Er, excuse me. He did have something to do with this,' said Miranda.

'He fucking slept with you then brutally fucking dumped you,' yelled Shaz.

'He didn't have to be so mean.'

'Darling, you know Mark's psychopathology,' mused Tom. 'He's avoidant. He emotionally flees at the first hint of pain. He'll come round.'

'I don't think so,' I said. 'Look at the engagement party. I just can't believe I was such an . . .'

A text pinged up on my phone.

DANIEL FUCKWIT DO NOT ANSWER

(I had recently made some changes in my address book.)

Everyone jumped in startlement and peered at the phone as if it contained a message from an Egyptian god released by the morning sun shining through a tiny hole in a pyramid onto an amulet.

DANIEL FUCKWIT DO NOT ANSWER
Jones, sorry about the phone cutting out
the other day. Could I possibly come over?

Then another.

```
DANIEL FUCKWIT DO NOT ANSWER
I shall, of course, be wearing wellington
boots and a full-body plastic cagoule.
```

'DON'T SEE HIM,' ordered Miranda bossily. ''Ere have we run out of wine?'

'I can't just *not see him*; he might be the father of my . . .'

'You should see him,' said Tom thoughtfully.

'Bus DON'TS sleeps wi' him.'

'She's goner get pregnant again.'

'Wis triplets,' slurred Shaz.

'SPECKLED triplets,' growled Miranda.

THURSDAY 19 OCTOBER

7 p.m. My flat. Daniel appeared at the top of the stairs holding a stylish bunch of flowers wrapped in edgy brown paper and tied with straw.

'Now, Jones, you are not to worry. I'm going to take care of everything.'

'You are?' I said suspiciously, letting him in.

'Of course, Jones. May not have been perfect in the past, but when the chips are down: perfect gentleman.'

'OK,' I said, brightening, as he flung himself down on the sofa in his immaculate suit.

'Christ, Jones, is this chocolate?' he said, pulling out something he'd just sat on.

'Sorry about that.'

'So, as I say, just tell me where to meet you and I'll come along and support and pay for the whole thing.'

'WHAT?'

'You're not going to keep it, are you? Christ, Jones, sorry. I just assumed in this situation . . .'

'OK, that's it! Out!' I said, pushing him towards the door. 'Oh, actually, there's one more thing, Daniel. The baby might not be yours.'

'I'm sorry?'

'She might not be yours. She might be Mark Darcy's.'

Daniel took a moment to digest this, then, with a flicker in his eye, said, 'Who was first, him or me?'

'Daniel! This actually is more important than you winning your centuries-old public-school row with Mark Darcy.'

'Jones, Jones, Jones. I'm sorry. You're right.' He came back into the flat, sighed dramatically, then made a show of composing himself.

'I want to do this: be there for you, new man, come to the scan, whatever.'

'You are so never going to turn up to a scan.'

'I am.'

'You're not.'

'I AM.'

'You so aren't. You'll have a date with some eighteen-year-old lingerie model and flake on me.'

'I am going to come to the scan.'

'*So* don't believe you.'

'I bloody well am. I'm coming to the scan of my child and you can't stop me. Right, Jones, I have to go. I've got a . . . got a . . .'

'Date?'

'No, no, no: publishing meeting. Text me when and where and I'll be there with a gown and rubber gloves.'

8.10 p.m. Sat down, staring crazily into space with one eye closed and the other open. Was this just about rivalry with Mark Darcy, or did Daniel actually want to be a father?

Thought back to when I was dating (i.e., being permanently messed around by) Daniel and when my old friend Jude (now a hotshot banker in New York) was being messed around by Vile Richard, and Shazzer started ranting about 'Emotional Fuckwittage', which, she claimed, was spreading like wildfire amongst men in their thirties.

8.20 p.m. Just looked back at my diary of Shazzer's rant:

As women glide from their twenties to thirties, the balance of power subtly shifts. Even the most outrageous minxes lose their nerve, wrestling with the first twinges of existential angst: fears of dying alone and being found three weeks later half eaten by an Alsatian. And men like Richard play on the chink in the armour to wriggle out of commitment, maturity, honour and the natural progression of things between a man and a woman.

You can hardly call what Daniel had just said the natural progression of things between a man and a woman.

But could it be true that even fuckwits like Daniel *do* want children? They just can't ever get past their fuckwittage to make a decision?

The strange thing about all this is all through my thirties I've thought that children were something you had to sort of *wrangle* men into. Almost something you had to pretend *not* to want in order to keep a man, otherwise they'd run off screaming.

Maybe that was the difference between Singletons like me, Miranda and Shazzer and Smug Marrieds like Magda. Smug Married women never had that insecurity or ambivalence, and went for a realistic choice and some sort of balanced lifestyle transaction as soon as possible: never even entertaining the thought that a man would *not* want to have children with them?

8.30 p.m. Emboldened by my new revelation, even if not exactly sure what it precisely was, I sent Mark a text.

```
Mark, I understand how complicated this
is, but I am having a scan on Monday 23
October at 5 p.m. and if you wanted to
come I would like that very much.
```

8.32 p.m. Staring fixedly at blank phone.

8.33 p.m. No reply from Mark.

8.34 p.m. Still no reply from Mark.

8.35 p.m. But what if he does reply yes? What do I do about Daniel? What if I tell Mark that Daniel wants to come and Mark still says yes? What if I don't tell Mark about Daniel on the assumption that Daniel's never going to turn up anyway, and then Daniel does turn up?

8.45 p.m. Realise there have been so many times in my life when I've fantasised about going to a scan with Mark or Daniel: just not both at the same time.

9 p.m. Right. Broccoli. We're eating too many cheesy potatoes and we need to enter different food groups. Broccoli is a Crossover Food that embraces more than one essential food group. Like pomegranates.

9.30 p.m. Baby hates broccoli. Am going to have cheesy potato.

10 p.m. Still no text from Mark.

FRIDAY 20 OCTOBER

6 p.m. *Sit Up Britain* studios. '*Sit Up Britain!*' said Miranda, to camera, in her urgent newsreader voice. 'The hard-hitting news show that makes you shit up!'

BONG.

'Did I just say shit up?' said Miranda, as the title

footage showed reporters striding around the globe with determined expressions.

'Yes,' I whispered into her feed, glancing round to check that Peri Campos wasn't watching.

'Unpronounceable headline, anyway,' said Miranda, looking up at the camera for her next autocue. 'So my point is, what sort of MONSTER doesn't reply to a text inviting him to a scan?'

'Maybe he's in a meeting?'

'For FOUR DAYS? Sod him. And now – fascinators! Are they the new earrings?'

BONG.

'WTF?' said Miranda. 'Who wrote this rubbish? Who wears two fascinators?'

'Peri Campos wrote it,' I hissed, while shots whizzed by of the fascinator-adorned heads of Camilla and Kate and Princess Beatrice and Eugenie. 'Assisted by the man-bun youths who say "whoa" and "bro".'

'Ugh,' said Miranda. 'Go with Daniel, bro.'

'But his first reaction was to get rid of my baby.'

'At least he's coming up with the goods now, and he's a legit shag, bro. And protests in the Maghreb, spilling over to the London embassy.'

BONG.

'Oh my God, Bridget! Look at the clip.' There was a shot of crowds milling around in white robes outside a red-mud palace, a close-up of people shouting, and in the background, making his way through the crowds with Freddo, his Oxbridge assistant, was Mark Darcy.

9 p.m. My flat. Feeling much better now that there is a reason for Mark's silence. Have been reading *What to Expect When You're Expecting* and *We Need More Crossover Foods.* Am making Crossover Food muffins with broccoli in. I found them in a cookbook full of ingenious ways of trying to make children eat vegetables. Next I'm going to do chocolate mousse made with avocados.

9.15 p.m. Shit, shit, have just reached up to get a glass from the cupboard and dropped it. There was one big bit in the muffin mixture, but I got it out. Sure it will all be fine.

10 p.m. Still no text from Mark. Looks like it's just me and Daniel. Or more likely just me. Oh, goody, text.

```
DANIEL FUCKWIT DO NOT ANSWER
Still on for the big day, Jones. See you
tomorrow.
```

MONDAY 23 OCTOBER

5 p.m. Dr Rawlings's office. 'Ah! Is this Daddy?' Dr Rawlings bustled into the room, with an arch glance at Daniel and myself. 'Nice to finally see who you are. Right, let's get started, shall we?'

She folded up my top to reveal my bump.

'Good God, Jones,' said Daniel. 'You look like a boa constrictor who's eaten a goat.'

'Wait!' said Dr Rawlings, poised with the ultrasound

thingy in the air and starting to smile at Daniel incredulously. 'I recognise that voice. You're on the television,
aren't you? Didn't you do that travel show?'

'Yeeees, *The Smooth Guide*,' murmured Daniel, at
which Dr Rawlings went all giggly and fluttery.

'Daniel Cleaver! *The Smooth Guide*! Oh, we used to
love it. We used to watch it every single week. We absolutely hooted when you were rolling around in the mud
with those girls in Thailand.'

'Can we look at the baby, please?' I said, thinking, 'Is
there no area of life impervious to celebrity culture?'

'Oh my goodness, wait till I tell everyone,' Dr Rawlings carried on. 'I say, you couldn't do me an autograph,
could you?' She put down the probe and started looking
around for a piece of paper. 'Here! Prescription pad! Perfect! Put something funny.'

Saw a glint come into Daniel's eye. Oh God. Was he
going to draw a penis or something?

'What are you up to now, Daniel? Any new shows
coming up?'

'I'm bringing out a novel,' he said, writing something
on the prescription pad.

'Oh, super! Is it funny?' she asked flirtatiously.

'No, no, not at all, actually. It's a literary thing. It's
called *The Poetics of Time*. It's an existential study of—'

'Right! Better get on,' said Dr Rawlings, clearly even
more quickly bored by *The Poetics of Time* than I was.
She glanced at the note Daniel had written for her and
collapsed in giggles.

'Oh dear, oh dear,' she said, wiping her eyes and

starting to rub lubricant on my stomach as if she was wiping something off the floor.

'Ding dong!' said Daniel. 'Dr Rawlings, could you possibly do that to me afterwards? My waistband has become increasingly tight of late. I seriously fear there may be something growing in there.'

'That's your penis, Daniel,' I said, drily, as Dr Rawlings collapsed in giggles again.

'OK, settle down now, Bridget. Settle down,' she said.

'*Me* settle down?'

'Shh! Let's listen to the heartbeat.'

She turned up the machine and a giant thumping boomed out. Daniel looked genuinely freaked out.

'Is everything all right in there?' he said. 'It sounds like a French high-speed train.'

'Tip-top shape. Right! Let's look at the screen. Oh, there's the little hand! Look! And, oh! There's the penis!'

I sat bolt upright.

'Penis? She's got a penis? My little girl has got a penis?'

Somehow I'd been absolutely convinced that the baby was a girl. You know how a mother just *knows*?

'Yes, you see it there? Pretty big.'

'Like father like son,' purred Daniel.

'I don't want a great big penis inside me!'

'First time I've ever heard that from you, Jones. Oh, look, look he's rubbing his nose with his little hands.'

'Oh, he's trying to wave,' I said. 'Hello, sweetheart. It's Mummy, it's your mummy, hello!' I was completely overcome. It was the best thing I'd ever seen in my life ever, apart from the last scan, which was also the best thing I'd ever seen in my life ever.

I looked at Daniel to see that he too was choked with emotion. He looked as if he was about to cry.

'Jones,' he said, fumbling for my hand. 'It's our little boy.'

We departed from the scan in Daniel's newly valeted Mercedes, the pale grey interior still smelling faintly of sick. Daniel was driving incredibly slowly, so much so that cars were honking and swerving past us.

'I think you could go a tiny bit faster,' I ventured, immediately feeling like I had catapulted from a person from *The Jerry Springer Show* to the sort of Smug Married who passive-aggressively back-seat drives with her husband.

Daniel put his foot on the accelerator, hit a speed bump, and braked.

'Oh Christ! Oh Christ! Has he fallen out? Is he all right? Jesus, Jones! Move the seat belt. Move the seat belt off him now or it'll squash his head.'

'Oh no! Will it?' I cried, taking off the seat belt. 'Have we squashed him? But how are we going to drive him home if I can't wear the seat belt?'

We both looked at each other, panicked, like seven-year-olds.

Somehow we made it back to the flat, me holding the seat belt away from my bump, Daniel growing increasingly quiet.

I took the seat belt off as gently and carefully as I could as we pulled up, to ensure it didn't ping back and squash the baby.

'You go on up,' said Daniel. 'I'll park the car. Make sure your phone's on in case anything else happens.'

I took out the phone as Daniel roared away, remembering I'd turned it off for the scan, to find a string of texts from Mark.

> **MARK DARCY**
> Bridget, I'm just getting on a plane back to Heathrow and have got your texts. Is the scan still scheduled for today? I shall try to be there if we're on time.

> **MARK DARCY**
> Just landed. Am going to rush over. Where is the scan?

> **MARK DARCY**
> Which hospital are you in?

> **MARK DARCY**
> Bridget? Please don't sulk. I've been in North Africa with no signal for four days.

As I walked very, very carefully towards the flat, to avoid the baby falling out, I saw a familiar figure in a dark overcoat approaching from the opposite direction.

'Mark!' I said, hurrying towards him.

His face broke into a grin. 'I couldn't find you. Didn't you get my texts? How did it go?'

There were footsteps behind me.

'Darcy! What the devil are you doing here?' said Daniel. 'We just came back from the scan, didn't we, Bridge?'

Daniel attempted to put his arm round me. I wriggled free, but then, to my total horror, he took out the scan photo and showed it to Mark.

'What do you think? Handsome little devil, isn't he?'

Mark didn't look at the photo. 'I would have been there, but I was in the Maghreb.'

'Ah, yes, I know it well. Little belly-dancing club in Old Compton Street?'

Mark lunged towards him.

'OK, Mrs Darcy, keep your wig on.'

'Stop it,' I said. 'Don't fight. I already have one child inside me.'

'You're right,' said Mark. 'We need to discuss this calmly, as adults. Can we come inside?'

'If only,' said Daniel, 'we'd thought of asking that before.'

My flat. 'Anyone want a cup of tea?' I said brightly, as if I was Mum in Grafton Underwood and the vicar had just popped round for some butterfly buns and a sherry.

The two men were looking at each other sideways, like US presidential candidates about to kick off one of their slagging matches thinly disguised as debates.

'Darce,' said Daniel, in a kindly tone, 'I understand

how emasculating this must feel, after all those years of everyone saying you were firing blanks.'

Mark started pushing him towards the balcony.

'Darcy hasn't got the soldiers,' sing-songed Daniel.

'What are you DOING?' I said as Mark shoved him outside and locked the French windows.

'Maybe he'll jump,' muttered Mark.

'Will you two stop bickering and grow up – it's like having two children,' I said, bustling around with the tea. 'Mark, let Daniel back in.' I had literally turned into Magda and was on the point of saying, 'Mummy will smack, she will smack, she will smack.'

'Grow up?' said Daniel, coming back from the balcony. 'You slept with both of us in frankly alarmingly quick succession like a member of Generation Z.'

I sat down wearily at the kitchen table. Was this what it was going to be like being a mother? Preparing people MEALS and GRINDING MYSELF TO THE BONE while they squabble and fight? Suddenly remembered I had forgotten to put the kettle on. Maybe I could serve them the Crossover Food muffins?

'Look, the situation is far from ideal,' said Mark. 'But it is, perhaps, an opportunity for us all to look at our behaviour and responsibilities, and act with everyone's best—'

'Right, great, Mother Superior. Is one going to start singing "Climb Every Mountain" now?'

'Teas up!' I trilled. 'And I've got home-made muffins!'

Daniel and Mark looked at each other, more horrified than by anything before.

The three of us sat at the kitchen table, struggling to eat the, by my own admission, disgusting Crossover broccoli muffins.

Suddenly, Mark started choking. He pulled a large piece of glass out of his mouth.

'What's this?'

'Oh shit! I broke a glass when I was doing the mixture. I thought I'd got it all out. Are you all right?'

Daniel leapt up and SPAT his muffin into the sink. He picked up another piece of broken glass and held it out. 'I feel like my life is disintegrating before my very eyes. Is this what parenthood is? Vomit in my car? Chocolate on my suits? Broccoli-and-glass-chip muffins in my stomach?'

'I'm so sorry, I'm so sorry, I thought I'd got it all out. I've just made a terrible mess of everything. I can't do this.'

I slumped at the table, head on my arms. I just wanted it all to stop. Apart from the baby.

Mark came over and put his arms round me. 'It's all right, it's all right. You're doing fantastically well.'

'You haven't actually killed us, 'said Daniel, freakishly clearing out the sink. 'Unless powdered glass is at this moment puncturing all our intestines.'

'It has actually been a near-death experience for us all,' said Mark, starting to laugh.

'So now can we all sort of unite and pull together?' I said, hopefully.

'Push, surely,' said Daniel.

Everyone settled down then, and we drank our tea nicely like the sort of well-behaved family you see in old-fashioned movies from the 1950s: unlike modern TV shows where the children snap out sassy and slightly insulting lines at their gay parents written by sophisticated writers' rooms in Hollywood.

'What about our parents?' I said, suddenly sitting bolt upright.

'We have to tell them, of course,' said Mark.

Oh God, I thought. The village! Grafton Underwood! Admiral and Elaine Darcy! Mum, Una and Mavis Enderbury!

'Parents?' said Daniel.

'Yes,' said Mark. 'Do you have parents?'

'Not that I'm ever going to tell.'

'Interesting. It is the Queen's visit rehearsal next Saturday, Bridget. I understand you are planning to be there?'

'You mean we should tell them there?' I said, horrified.

'Separately, privately, of course.'

'You can't tell I'm pregnant yet, can you? I can't go if everyone in the village is going to notice.'

There was a slight pause, then they said:

'No.'

'Nope.'

'Can't tell at all.'

'I seriously think the baby's going to come out flat, Jones.'

EIGHT

FAMILY VALUES

Grafton Underwood: Queen's visit rehearsal. 'Family Values!' Mark's father, Admiral Darcy, was bellowing into the microphone.

The entire village was assembled, together with the Lord Mayor, and representatives from the Palace, who were checking out the scene.

'Family Values and Village Life shall be our theme,' the Admiral thundered on, 'as, for the first time in her thousand-year history, the Ethelred Stone, and its gracious vestibule, the village of Grafton Underwood, welcomes a reigning monarch to our strawy rooftops!'

'Strawy rooftops!' said Uncle Geoffrey, way too loudly. 'Is he on the sauce already?'

I glanced at Mark, on the other side of the group, who was trying not to laugh. We had arrived in Mark's car, driven by his driver, but I'd jumped out first, round the corner from Mum's house, so we could appear to arrive separately. We didn't want to set everyone off just yet.

'And today,' Admiral Darcy went on, 'we are honoured to have with us the Clerk to the Northamptonshire Lieutenancy here to approve our plans for the visit of Her Majesty, and guide us in our protocol for the Reception Committee, and for the seating plan.'

'Admiral.' Mavis Enderbury raised her hand. 'Can I just ejaculate for a moment over the luncheon?'

'She just means she wants to sit next to the bloody Queen,' Mum hissed to Una.

As the speech ended and everyone started to disperse, Mum turned and spotted me. Her eyes went straight to my boobs and bump.

'Bridget,' she said. 'Are you *preggy*?'

Gaaah! Was it that obvious already? But Mark, Daniel, Tom, Miranda and Shazzer all said you couldn't tell.

'She is, she's preggy, Pam!' said Una.

Everyone was staring.

'Do you have to say "preggy"?' I said, queasily.

'Oh, Bridget!' said Mum, delighted. 'Oh, what *perfect* timing!' She suddenly looked coy. 'Is it Mark's? He's here, you know. We were all just saying, now that he's got divorced from that frightful intellectual woman, maybe you two had seen sense at last. Do you remember how you used to play with him in the paddling pool? Bridget, is it Mark's?'

'Maybe. I mean, there's at least a fifty per cent chance.'

Saw Mavis Enderbury listening in with an evil look of triumph in her eye.

'A *fifty per cent chance*?' said Mum. 'Bridget! Did you have a threesome?'

Back at Mum and Dad's house there were tears and drama.

'I've waited all your adult life for you to have a little baby and now you have to do it like this, in front of the cream of Grafton Underwood and Mavis Enderbury. I've never been so humiliated in my entire life.'

'But, Pam,' Dad said gently, 'it's a baby. It's our grand-child. You've always wanted a grandchild.'

'Not like this,' wailed Mum. 'This isn't how it was sup-posed to be.'

'Have you had it checked out?' blurted Una. 'I mean, at your age it could come out a mongol.'

'Una!' I said. 'You cannot say "mongol" in this day and age. Mum, I did not mean to embarrass you. I was led to believe by reliable sources that the bump was not visible to the untrained eye. I came to the Ethelred Stone because you've been going on and on about it and I wanted to support you. I was going to tell you quietly, here, just with our family. It's a baby. It's a life. It's your grandson. I thought you'd be happy. If you're going to be like this, I'm off.'

As I stomped back to where Mark's car was waiting, I passed Admiral and Elaine Darcy's manor house and heard raised voices behind the tall privet hedge.

'What kind of carry-on is this, boy? We're not docked in some Caribbean port! You'll put the whole Royal Whatsit in jeopardy and make us look like bloody fools!'

'My dear Admiral . . .' I heard Elaine Darcy remon-strate.

'Look at me when I'm talking to you, boy. What's the matter with you?'

'Father, I've explained to you the reality of the situa-tion, and I'm afraid that is all I have to say. Goodbye.'

There was a pause. I heard Mark's footsteps scrunch-ing away across the gravel, then the Admiral continued,

'Why can't he just stay married and bloody reproduce like everyone else? Do you think he's queer?'

'Well, you wanted to send him to Eton, dear.'

'What? What are you bloody talking about?'

'I'll never forgive myself.'

'For what? What, woman?'

'All those nannies, boarding schools: for delegating the upbringing of my only son.'

There was a silence.

'Anyway,' said the Admiral, eventually. 'Jolly good. Stiff Upper Lip.'

Dad came hurrying along and caught me skulking along the hedge.

'Let's sit down, pet.'

We walked along a bit from the Darcys' house and sat on the grassy bank.

'Don't worry about your mum. You know how she is: mad as a bucket, mad as a snake. She'll come round when she's got used to the idea.'

We sat quietly for a moment. You could hear the stream, the birds, voices in the distance: the old, simple scene.

'It's the expectation which undoes everyone. Every time. It should be like this, it should be like that. The trick is to deal with what is. You always wanted a baby, now, didn't you?'

'Well, always in about three years' time for about two hours,' I said sheepishly. 'But I realise now, yes, I did.'

'And now you're going to get your baby. And he's going

to be the luckiest baby in the world because he's got you as his mother. There won't be a more loving, kind mother than you – think of the fun that little chap's going to have with you. Now you go out there, do your best, and don't get caught up in everyone else's nonsense. It'll turn out fine, I promise you.'

Dad walked with me to Mark's car, with the waiting driver, promising he wouldn't tell Mum. When Mark appeared, looking upset and shaken, Dad clapped him on the shoulder in a manly way and gave him a conspiratorial smile. But he didn't say anything. That's the brilliance of Dad. He knew Mark would hate it, and that he didn't need to.

As the car purred off, I took a leaf out of Dad's book and simply put my head on Mark's shoulder and closed my eyes. As I drifted off to sleep, I'm sure I heard Mark whisper, 'Even if the baby does turn out to be Daniel's, I still want to be his dad.'

SATURDAY 4 NOVEMBER

5 p.m. Just got back from baby shopping in John Lewis department store with Mark and Daniel. They always say if anything really bad happens you should go to John Lewis, because nothing really bad ever happens in John Lewis.

*

Mark was holding a huge pile of baby books and a box of muslin baby blankets that said 'Huggy Swaddle'.

'Swaddling?' said Daniel incredulously, holding a miniature Chelsea football outfit. 'You're into swaddling?'

'It can be effective,' said Mark, with the air of an expert witness who had been called on to advise on military intervention versus peacekeeping, 'if it's not too tight.'

'. . . and you're an Egyptian peasant in the fourth century BC.'

'It promotes sleep,' said Mark, picking up a wipe-warmer, as if hardly aware of Daniel's presence.

'What? When they're strapped to a board? Isn't that a little Abu Ghraib?'

'Yes, you have no sense whatsoever as to what is and isn't appropriate in terms of what you apparently consider a "joke". Presumably, you would have the child screaming all night till he falls asleep, drunk on teaspoons of whisky.'

'You take that back!'

They were quickly removed from the store by the John Lewis security team. Nothing bad is ever allowed to happen in John Lewis. Sadly, it is not so everywhere.

SUNDAY 12 NOVEMBER

5 p.m. My flat. Just back from childbirth class. Mark rushed up late, talking on the phone, briefcase in hand,

and acknowledged Daniel and myself with a brief nod, still talking on the phone.

'Turn it off, Darce, there's a good chap,' said Daniel.

We signed in at reception and burst through the double doors to find an instructor in front of a table with a rubber model of the bottom half of a woman. Couples were sitting in lines at tables, each of them trying to put a nappy on a plastic baby.

'Ah!' said the instructor. 'Welcome! Find yourselves a baby in the bin there!'

There was just one brown plastic baby doll left in the bin.

'If we'd got here on time we could have had a white baby,' whispered Daniel, to appalled stares.

'Daniel,' I hissed. 'Shut urrrrp!'

'Right!' said the instructor, smoothing it over. 'Who have we here? Mark? Daniel? You're our second same-sex couple today.'

Everyone applauded politely as Daniel smirked at Mark's expression.

'And Bridget? You're the surrogate? Welcome!'

Didn't think it was a good idea to explain at that particular juncture, so I just smiled vaguely while everyone fussed around rearranging the chairs.

'No,' said Mark suddenly, 'we are not a couple.'

There was a moment's silence while everybody stared.

'Right . . . sooo . . . ?' said the instructor. 'So you and Bridget are a couple?'

'No.'

'So Daniel and Bridget are . . .'

'None of us are a couple,' I said. 'I slept with both of them and I don't know which one is—'

'Oh! So you both opted for actual intercourse with the surrogate! That's unusual! Anyway, all comers welcome here!'

'"Comers" being the operative word,' remarked Daniel.

'Let's carry on, shall we?' She held up the rubber gynaecological model. 'What's the opening of the uterus called? Anyone tell me?'

Daniel shot his hand up: 'The vagina!'

'Um, no . . . actually.'

'The cervix,' said Mark.

'The cervix. Exactly! And the *opening* to the cervix?'

'The vagina!' said Daniel triumphantly.

'Yes! Or, as we call it, the birth canal, or, for Baby, the exit into a new world.'

'Always two ways of looking at anything,' said Daniel.

The instructor was now holding up a plastic baby and the rubber cut-in-half-woman. Honestly, how did any normal relationship ever survive a childbirth class?

'So! Let's have a look at what actually happens when Baby's finally on the way. So the birth canal needs to open up.' She pushed the baby down head first into the rubber half-woman. 'Can I have a volunteer to play doctor? How about you, Daniel?'

'. . . since opening up vaginas has been your life's work,' murmured Mark.

'OK! So! Doctor! You put your hand in here.'

She guided Daniel's hand up into the rubber lady's

'birth canal'. 'And Baby pushes down from here. Can you feel Baby?'

'Frightfully sorry,' said Daniel, wriggling his hand in the rubber birth canal. 'I can't seem to reach it.'

Mark smirked as Daniel tried to shove his hand further up while the instructor shoved the doll further down.

'Ugh,' said the instructor, suddenly revealing a snappy side. 'This happens every *sugaring* time. I keep asking for another one. That's the National Health for you. Nobody's vagina is this small.'

'You've obviously never been to the Ping Pong Puck in Bangkok,' said Daniel.

'Oh. My. God!' said the instructor, looking at Daniel disbelievingly. 'Oh my God. You're the man from that travel show! Aren't you? I saw you on that programme from Bangkok! It was hilarious! Daniel Cleaver!'

Everyone was now looking at Daniel excitedly.

'Are you doing another show?'

'Well, actually, no,' said Daniel, trying to extract his arm from the birthing canal. 'I've just written a novel, actually. It's called *The Poetics of*—'

'Right, that's it,' said Mark. 'This is intolerable. I'm leaving.'

The three of us stood outside in the street with rain drizzling down and lorries and buses roaring past.

'You're an imbecile, you're a child,' Mark was saying furiously to Daniel.

'Well, she said to ask questions.'

'I deeply resent being placed in these idiotic situations with such a ludicrous—'

'Well, get out of it, then, Mrs D. Everyone knows you haven't got the soldiers anyway. Firing blanks for years.'

'You take that back,' said Mark.

'The dominant sperm conquers all.'

Mark made as if to punch him.

'Mark, stop!' I said.

The two of them stood, squaring off like boxers.

I literally couldn't take it any more. Neither of them noticed as I saw a cab approaching with its light on. 'Bye!' I said as it pulled up. 'Talk to you later.'

'Wait! Bridget!' said Mark.

'I'm just tired,' I said. 'Thanks for coming, guys. Talk to you later.'

When I looked out of the back window they seemed to have stopped fighting, but Daniel was talking intently to Mark. Then Mark suddenly turned on his heel and strode away.

10 p.m. My flat. Ooh, goody! Doorbell. Maybe Mark!

It was not Mark, but a courier with a letter from Mark.

Mark is literally the only person who still writes letters, in ink, on embossed paper.

Dear Bridget,

The current situation cannot sustain. I have stated my feelings for you and the baby, but it has now become clear that I have no place in this ludicrous and unbridled scenario. My concern for your well-being is tempered by the knowledge that, had you been honest and clear to me much earlier in this situation, a great deal of distress and confusion could have been avoided.

The priority now is for you not to become embroiled in further antics, but simply to rest and take care of the unborn child. If I can in any way offer financial assistance or support, you need only let me know and I will honour that commitment.

Yours ever,
Mark

Nine

Chaos and Disorder

10.15 a.m. *Sit Up Britain* **office.** Just got into work. I can't do this. I absolutely cannot do a day's work with the following things inside me:

1) Increasingly large baby asking for baked potatoes, cheese, gherkins and, suddenly, vodka.
2) A completely confused and broken heart. Why did Mark write that letter? Just when it had all been so sweet on the car journey from Grafton Underwood. Why? What happened? Why isn't he answering my texts? Maybe he actually thinks I'm trashy and slutty and Daniel reminds him of the part of me he doesn't like.

Furtively FaceTimed Tom under the desk.

'You're not trashy or slutty,' said Tom on FaceTime. 'You're a top news producer and you're practically a nun. You need to play At Least. You know? That thing you showed me, when I was being tortured by Pretentious Jerome? At least? At least I have this, that or the other. Makes it seem better?'

'Yes! Yes!' I said, brightening. 'Thanks, Tom.'

Clicked FaceTime off.

FaceTime popped up again: Tom.

'Bridge, just a note to self. Don't FaceTime anyone again from that angle.'

Tom disappeared, then popped up again on FaceTime: 'Am I a horrible person?'

'Bridget, get on,' said Richard Finch, walking past my desk and glancing at my boobs.

Quickly texted Tom, 'No, nice person,' then started typing furiously and staring intently at the screen: for all the world as if I was working on the day's running order.

AT LEAST
I'm having a baby.
It might be all right with Mark – it could just be a blip.
Daniel is still in the picture, so at least one father left.
Daniel might change.
I have my own flat.
I have my own car.
I have a lovely dad.
Mum might change and start being happy about the baby instead of obsessed with the Queen's visit.
I am surrounded by friends, both Singleton and Smug Married, like an extended, warm, Third World family.
I have a great job and no one, apart from Miranda, knows I am pregnant yet.

*

'They're fucking enormous,' came a loud whisper behind me.

'Whoa, bro. They're totally legit.'

'Look at this, Jordan. From this angle, against the sign, the tips used to be just teasing the *P* on *Sit Up Britain,* but now they're right across the *B.*'

'Yo. Sick, bro.'

'I mean they're fucking enor—'

'Whoa. Just, like totally boss, bro.'

I whirled round. It was Richard Finch whispering with one of the man-bun youths.

'What are you two talking about?'

'Nothing.'

'Richard! I know you were talking about my boobs.'

'I wasn't!'

'You were!'

'I wasn't!'

'It's sexism. It's harassment.'

'I was just remarking on a natural phenomenon,' said Richard. 'If you saw a double-decker bus which had doubled in size you'd be entitled to say something about it, wouldn't you?'

'I am not a bus, I am a human being. Anyway, excuse me, I have to pee.'

Richard Finch suddenly had one of those rare moments when a thought came into his head.

'Are you PREGNANT?' he yelled.

There was a loud silence. Turned to see that everyone was staring and Peri Campos had just come into the office.

It was all too much. The baby ejected his cheesy baked potato and cappuccino in protest and I threw up into the wastepaper basket in front of everyone.

8 p.m. My flat. These are the people who have been fired in Peri Campos's 'pruning'.

June on Reception (seventeen years at *Sit Up Britain*).

Harry the driver (eighteen years at *Sit Up Britain*).

Julian the floor manager. Yes, he kept forgetting to tell us we were on air, and couldn't tell 'camera right' from 'camera left', but he'd been studying the difference for twenty years.

As we all filed out of the meeting, Peri Campos called me aside.

'HR is familiar with employees getting pregnant when their jobs are in jeopardy. Though usually employees whose jobs are in jeopardy are too old to get pregnant. Anyway, don't think you can get away with any bullshit.'

She turned back to the room. 'Oi! You lot! One last thing! We're going to start an hour earlier in the mornings.'

Honestly! Everyone knows people in the media are supposed to start late because they're so bohemian and creative. I've booked the first slot at 8 a.m. for the scan on Thursday so I could be back at work by 11.

Oh come on, sure, it will be fine. Will be here by 9.30. Will be early!

Number of texts sent to Mark: 7. Number of replies from Mark: 0.

Just called Mark's office and got his Oxbridge assistant, Freddo.

'Arm yar,' said Freddo, in his resonant tenor. 'Arm. He won't be in the office for a couple of weeks. Off the radar.'

'Has he gone somewhere scary?'

'Just, arm, yup off the radar. Jolly good.'

That's odd. Ooh, text.

```
DANIEL FUCKWIT DO NOT ANSWER
All set for the scan tomorrow, Jones? See
how our little express train's coming
along?
```

Looks like it's just me and Daniel again. At least he remembered. Maybe he's changed.

8 a.m. Hospital waiting room. Daniel is not here.

8.10 a.m. Daniel is still not here. Oh God oh God oh God. I'm supposed to be at work in fifty minutes. Peri Campos will kill me, then eat me.

8.20 a.m. Receptionist just said, 'If you don't go in now you'll miss your slot.'

Was just gathering up my bags when Daniel burst in, bad mood written all over him (well, not literally, that would be weird).

'Traffic total hell, entire city bloody gridlocked. Why did you have to fix it so bloody early, Jones? Come on, let's get on with it. Where's Darcy, anyway?'

'He isn't here.'

Didn't seem a good idea to tell Daniel that Mark was out of the picture: rather like when you're trying to get everyone *behind an idea* at work, and if one person drops out, then they all do. Definitely am not going to tell him.

'No Darce?'

'Mark's not coming,' I blurted. 'He wrote me a letter. He doesn't want to join in any more.'

There was a momentary glint of triumph in Daniel's eye. 'It's the ego. Always the ego with Mrs Darcy.'

'What do you mean?'

'Nothing, nothing, just that childbirthing class.'

'You might have apologised,' I said.

'For what, Jones? It was jolly good fun. Everyone had a whale of a time except Mrs D. Don't have to treat the whole thing like it's an execution in a grungy prison in Arabia.'

The terrible thing was that Dr Rawlings had been called away to a delivery (assumed of another baby, not FedEx parcel). Found myself unexpectedly feeling jealous of the other baby and Dr Rawlings, almost as if she was cheating on me. And, worse, we had a male technician instead, so Daniel had no one to flirt with. All the energy seemed to have gone out of Daniel. Without Mark to compete with, he just seemed to be going through the motions.

I, meanwhile, was so overwhelmed with love and seeing how my little gorgeous sweetheart had grown, his round head, his little nose, his hands, that I totally forgot about the time.

'Gaaaaaah!' I said when we got out on the street. 'It's 9.15 – I was supposed to be at work fifteen minutes ago.'

'OK, OK. No need to overdo it. I'll take you to work,' said Daniel, adding under his breath, 'Never mind my galleys, my proofreading. *Sit Up Britain* must reign supreme.'

Car journey could only be described as tense. I was trying to mentally force the clock on the dashboard to go backwards, and move lorries and bicycles out of the way by the sheer power of thought, whilst realising we were half an hour past the moment when I was supposed to be at my desk. Daniel was preoccupied and twitching, playing with the controls on the car and suddenly zooming and braking, in a way that made me think I was going to be sick in it again.

When we got to the *Sit Up Britain* building, Daniel stayed sitting down, with the engine running. 'All right, then, Jones. Well, great to catch up.'

'"Great to catch up"?' I said.

'See you around.'

'"See you around"?'

'Jones, don't keep repeating everything I say like a parrot.'

'"Like a parrot"?'

'Jones.'

'I'm so confused. We just went to a scan together and now you're saying, "Great to catch up" and "See you around", as if we've just slept together.'

'Right, right,' said Daniel. 'It's all the same with you girls, isn't it? Just because we go to a scan together it doesn't mean we're going out together. It doesn't mean we have to get all serious and start having babies.'

'But we're already having a baby. That's why we went to the scan.'

'No, Jones,' he said. 'You're having a baby.'

I froze.

'Sorry, sorry,' he said. 'Look. I just don't think I can do this. I don't think I have the skill set.'

'What if it's yours?'

'I suppose I could try.'

'And if it isn't?'

'Well, that would change everything. Sorry, sorry, oh, come on, don't look at me like that, Jones. The point is, if we'd done it up the arse like I wanted to, none of this would have happened.'

'Daniel,' I said, getting out of the car. 'You can shove your mouth up your own bum. And if it was a choice of bringing up the baby with you or Peri Campos, I would choose Peri Campos.'

Beyond late, mind reeling from Daniel, I rushed up to the seventh floor, grabbed a sheaf of papers and held them in front of my stomach – to give a pleasing air of just having popped out to the scanner and not being late or pregnant at all – then walked casually into the office: to find Peri Campos conducting a meeting for the entire *Sit Up Britain* staff.

'It's wet, it's see-through and without it we'd DIE! Water!' she was yelling, strutting in front of a Smart Board while the youths in their man-buns sat up attentively at the front and the old guard sat sulkily at the back.

'Bridget, you're thirty-five minutes late, dated and boring. *Sit Up Britain* is dated and boring. The title is dated and boring. The staff is dated and boring. The content is dated and boring. We need tension, we need action, we need suspense. "They're small, they're fiercely powerful, they're potential killers and they're ALL OVER YOUR HOUSE!" Well?' She looked around expectantly.

'Ants!' said Jordan.

'Vacuums!' said Richard Finch.

'Vibrators?' said Miranda, as I spurted out laughing.

'It's batteries,' said Peri Campos, drily, 'for those of us who have any sort of tenuous handle on today's news. Bridget, see me in my office nine o'clock on Monday morning. That's nine o'clock – not three in the afternoon: not late.'

'It won't happen again, I promise.'

'Promise! I love that word because it raises so many talking points.'

'Please don't sack her,' said Richard Finch, looking at me and miming, 'Are you mad?'

8.30 p.m. My flat. Have sense of impending doom. Am about to be sacked, both the fathers hate me, everything is a mess, is Friday night and am all alone. Aloooooone!

AT LEAST

I'm having a baby.

It might be all right with Mark – it could just be a blip.

~~Daniel is still in the picture, so at least one father left.~~

~~Daniel might change.~~

I have my own flat.

I have my own car.

I have a lovely dad.

Mum might change and start being happy about the baby instead of obsessed with the Queen's visit.

I am surrounded by friends, both Singleton and Smug Married, like extended, warm, Third World family.

I have a ~~great~~ job (how long for?) and ~~no one, apart from Miranda, knows I am pregnant yet~~.

But, yes. I do have friends. Singletons to have fun and laugh with! There's no need to wallow. Will simply call Shazzer.

*

9 p.m. Conversation with Shazzer did not go well.

'Shaz? It's Bridget. Are you and Tom going out tonight?'

There was silence at the other end: the same silence as I used to emit when Magda called to see if she could come out with us and try, Smug-Marriedly and in vain, to share in our debauched Singleton fun.

'It's juss' – she sounded really drunk – 'we're in Hackney iss a bit kind of . . . out there?'

I bit my lip, tears pricking my eyelids. They didn't even ask me to come! I'm not a Singleton any more. I'm not a Smug Married. I'm a freak!

'Bridge. What's going on? Have we got cut off?'

'Why didn't you ask me to come?'

'Well . . . it's just, it's kind of a bit drunken and out there, you know, in your . . .'

'In my condition?'

I could hear squabbling in the background. Tom came on the phone, even more drunk than Shaz.

'It's bit messy, y'see,' he said. 'Miranda's . . .'

What? Miranda as well, there without asking me?

10 p.m. The thing is, when you feel isolated and alone, you have to 'reach out' to people, don't you?

10.05 p.m. Am going to 'reach out' by texting.

10.15 p.m. This is what have texted:

```
Magda, I feel so isolated and alone. I
cannot live the Singleton life any longer.
```

I need my Smug Married friends to support
me through this testing time.

Shazzer, I feel so isolated and alone.
Even though I am pregnant I am not a Smug
Mother and need the support of my Singleton friends to support me through this
testing time.

Mum, I feel isolated and alone. I cannot
get through this without the support of
my dear, dear mother. I need my mother to
support me through this testing time.

Mark, I feel isolated and alone. I cannot
go through this testing time without the
support of my dear, dear Mark. I need you
to support me through this testing time.

Daniel, I feel isolated and alone . . .

At that point I fell asleep.

11 a.m. My flat. Gaah! Woken by series of pinging and
ringing noises. Searched confusedly in duvet for source.

'Hello?' I said into the landline whilst fumbling for
still-pinging mobile.

'It's Magda. I was SO happy to get your text. We've all been DYING to chip in but we thought you were cosied up with your single friends and we were too boring. Anyway, you'll come to lunch in Portobello today? And then we'll start and get you sorted out. Of course everyone's going to give you endless insane advice, but not me.'

'Um, I'm still in bed, but—'

'In bed? Bridget, you are wearing a bra?'

'No. Should I?'

'Yes, or you'll end up with one breast under each arm, but nothing with underwiring.'

'Why not?' I said, thinking of my precious lift-and-separate lingerie collection.

'Underwiring crushes the milk ducts.'

'Hang on.' I answered the mobile. It was Tom.

'Tom! Hi! I'm on the other line. Call you back?'

'OK. Check your texts. We're meeting you in the Electric for Bloody Marys at 1 p.m.'

'Sorry, Mag,' I said, putting the landline back to my ear to find her still talking.

'Oh, and don't eat raw eggs.'

'Why would I eat raw eggs?'

'But, actually, the only advice really worth taking is not to lie down.'

'How can I not lie down?'

'Not on your back, because your main artery to your brain goes through your back.'

The mobile rang again. 'Darling, it's Mummy' – in tears – 'I had no idea you needed me. I thought you HATED me, it's been so . . .'

'Magda, I have to go. Mum is on the other line.'

'OK, see you in the Electric at one.'

Returned to the sound of Mum sobbing into the phone. 'Darling, I thought you were on no-speaks. I'm so glad you need me, darling. Anyway, we're coming down to Debenhams tomorrow afternoon, so will you come too and we can go shopping?'

'I'd love to, but—'

The landline rang.

'Mum, I've got to go, I'll call you back later.'

Magda again: 'The only other thing I was going to say is don't go swimming because it puts a strain on the uterus.'

I glanced down at my texts: a stream of placatory blandishments from Tom, Shaz and Miranda. We were all supposed to be meeting in the Electric at one o'clock, but wait . . .

'. . . oh, and if your hair starts falling out,' Magda was continuing, 'just rub a bit of engine oil in your scalp. Anyway, better get moving. See you in the Electric at one! Woney and Mufti are coming!'

'Um . . .' I thought, panicking wildly. I couldn't have the Smug Mothers turning up at the Electric at the same time as Tom, Miranda and Shazzer.

'The Electric's a bit noisy, could we make it at two . . . at Café 202?'

'Oh,' she said, huffily. 'Well. I've told Mufti and Woney now, but . . . OK yes. See you there.'

Just before I left I heard my email ping.

```
Sender: Peri Campos
Subject: Meeting Monday at 9
Be in my office at 9 on Monday, bringing
with you six breaking news stories which
are not dated or stultifyingly boring with
appropriate headlines, in format we dis-
cussed Friday.
```

Portobello Road, Notting Hill. Felt heady and freeing to be in the scruffy glamour and crowds of Portobello again: overpriced delis, flower shops and designer cashmere stores now mixed up with the betting shops and stalls selling street-cred hats and vegetables that have been there for years.

It was rather like being a celebrity, being pregnant, now that it was starting to show: cars screeching to a halt at zebra crossings, people giving up their seats on the tube, everyone stopping me and asking the same questions.

'Is it a boy or a girl?'

'When's it due?'

Of course, I was *terribly* gracious with my fans. Rather like the Queen, only pregnant and younger and not about to sit next to my mum in Grafton Underwood.

Reached the Electric feeling jolly, to find Shazzer slumped with her head on one of the outdoor tables. 'Hi! Shaz!' I said.

She emitted a slight groaning sound. 'I'm SO hung-over,

can you order me a Bloody Mary? I can't move my head.'

'Where are Tom and Miranda?'

'I dunno. Miranda hooked up with someone. And I think Tom was goner come straight here from wherever he went to, but I'm furious with him because . . .'

Oh God. It was already 1.15 p.m. – what about Magda? I mean, maybe I could be a tiny bit late?

Went inside to order a Bloody Mary and a mint tea. Came out to see Tom, dishevelled and unshaven, walking towards us with the determined air of a man being made to walk a straight line by a policeman who's pulled him over.

'Oh my God,' he said, joining Shazzer and crashing his head onto the table, reeking of tequila.

'They're wrecked, they're shag-drunk and they're all over your table! Tom and Shazzer!' said Miranda, bouncing up with a spring in her step, looking fresh and youthful.

'Aren't you hung-over?' I said, joining them at the table.

'Hung-over? No! Sex was my Friday-night drug of choice! Did you get the email from Peri Campos? Glass of white burgundy!' she said flirtatiously to the waiter, who had miraculously instantly appeared. She glanced, horrified, at my mint tea. 'And another glass of wine for Bridget, and bring us some food.'

'I can't, I'm pregnant,' I said, as Miranda ordered random food.

'No, no! Breaking news from Netdocbam!.com. Two

glasses of wine a week is GOOD FOR THE BABY. "It's wet, it's formerly toxic, and it's all over your foetus!"'

'REALLY?' I said, brightening. This was a double joy: a headline and a drinky.

'Shhh,' said Tom. 'You're hurting my head.'

Mmmm. Crisp, cold white wine was so delicious.

'So, want to know my other story?' said Miranda, sipping her drink. '"They're small, they're totally incontinent and they MAKE YOU DEPRESSED – babies!"'

'What?' said Shazzer, sitting bolt upright and shooting a look at Tom.

'Yup,' said Miranda smugly. 'Survey in next month's *Psychiatry Last Week Today.*'

'How did you get next month's *Psychiatry Last Week Today?*' said Tom from his prone position.

'Contacts, bro.'

'Please don't say "bro",' I said.

'Apparently all these years women have been *brainwashed* into thinking they're depressed because they don't have children, whereas apparently women who give up their careers to have children are more depressed than women who keep their careers and don't have children.'

'You SEE, Tom?' said Shazzer, adding, 'Tom's decided to adopt a baby. Jumping ship, jumping on the bandwagon.'

'Shazzer, shut up, it was a secret,' said Tom, furious.

I was staring at Miranda, aghast.

'Oh come on, you don't have to take any notice of an article. All surveys are bollox, but it's a headline for

Monday. They're passive-aggressive: "Oh, oh, look at me, I can't do anything, help me," and they ruin your life – babies!'

'Exactly! It's all propaganda!' crowed Shaz as I took a giant gulp of wine, remembering how much better it made one feel, and also wanting to have another one and a packet of Silk Cut. Started tucking into my goat's cheese toastie.

'All these years we've been BRAINWASHED into thinking we were depressed because we haven't got children, whereas, in fact, we weren't depressed at all!' Shazzer ranted gleefully.

'But, er, we were,' said Tom.

'No. We just THOUGHT we were because society made us believe we'd suffered an unbearable loss, whereas in fact people who make a conscious decision not to have children are not depressed at all,' said Shazzer.

'Hurrah!' I said, out of pure habit. 'Childless Singletons! Hurrah!'

'Bridget! What are you doing here? I thought you were meeting *us* for lunch.'

Gaaah! It was Magda and Mufti. Mufti was pushing a pram containing a baby and festooned with a scary amount of baby-clobber.

'Are you drinking WINE?'

I leapt to my feet guiltily, knocking the wine over with my stomach.

'She can't drink wine! She can't drink wine!' said Mufti.

'Honestly, you Singletons are completely irresponsible,' said Magda. 'She's coming with us. Bridget, come on.'

'Is that goat's cheese?' said Mufti. 'You're eating GOAT'S CHEESE?'

Woney suddenly appeared, also with a pram but no baby in it. 'What are you doing here – we thought we were meeting in Café 202. We've bought you a Bugaboo stroller!'

'Oh, thank you,' I gushed, looking doubtfully at the giant pram. How was I going to even get it up the stairs?

'Oh my God, you're enormous,' said Woney. 'I thought you were only a few months. You'll have to stop piling it on or you'll have a terrible delivery.'

Magda squeezed my hand and whispered, 'Take no notice of Woney – she spent so much time on her feet she got varicose veins in her labia,' at which Shazzer smirked.

'It's a girl!' said Mufti. 'It's a girl! Look how low-slung she's carrying.'

'No, it's not, it's a boy. Look how bloated her boobs are.'

'A boy? A boy? She's completely lopsided,' said Mufti. 'Completely lopsided.'

'OK, stop,' said Magda. 'We're here to help Bridget, not torture her. Guess what? We've found you a nanny: Eastern European. She's got a degree in Neuroscience from the University of Vilnius.'

'Have you found out who the father is?' said Woney. 'You can't have a baby without a father.'

'Look,' growled Tom, breathing alcohol fumes. 'It's

positively archaic to be living with two heterosexual parents of opposite sexes.'

'Wouldn't want to saddle a baby with that sort of social stigma,' said Shaz. Miranda was ignoring everyone, swiping on Tinder.

'I think you lot might be the tiniest bit bitter,' said Mufti. 'Bitter.'

'Why, because we didn't make a materialistic grab for any solvent man in sight when we hit thirty?' said Shaz.

'No, but maybe that's why you're childless and single.'

'Are you the one who got varicose veins in her labia?' rasped Shazzer.

Whole thing erupted into a terrible shouting match. Ended up being swept away by Magda, with the new giant gift pram – a somewhat weird accessory without a baby in it – while Magda went on and on about how it was going to be fine when I got my new nanny who was a friend of *her* nanny, Audrona, who had a degree in Aeronautical Engineering.

A very beautiful girl, who looked like the sort of Eastern European model/princess Daniel would stand me up at a scan for, was heading towards us pushing the identical Bugaboo stroller.

'Nice pram!' I said, suddenly thinking the bonding over the overpriced baby accessory might catapult me into a new glamorous Smug Mother strata.

'Nice baby!' she said, in an accent, looking into my pram – then looked at me oddly, since there clearly was no baby.

'Still cooking!' I said, patting my bump. 'But yours is adorable.'

The baby was indeed adorable – and yet oddly fa—

'Mama,' said the baby.

'Molly!' said Magda. 'That's my baby – what are you doing with my fucking baby?'

People were starting to stare as Magda struggled with the complex Bugaboo strapping arrangements to get Molly out of the pram, yelling, 'You've stolen my baby!'

'No! Do not be cross, Mrs Carew!' said the model/princess. 'Audrona has job interview. She asked me to take Molly. I have master's degree in Psychology and Early Childhood Development. She is fine, see?'

SUNDAY 19 NOVEMBER

2 p.m. My flat. Have spent most of day scouring newspapers for stories, which can turn into Peri Campos riddle-me-ree headlines for bloody meeting tomorrow:

'They're slimy, they're creepily silent – and they're lurking in your arugula – frogs!'

'They're hexagonal, they suddenly change their form and they gouge out your eyes – umbrellas!'

3 p.m. This is hopeless. This is ridiculous. Ooh, text.

*

3.05 p.m. A miracle! It's from Mark!

```
MARK DARCY
Bridget, I am mortified to hear that you
are isolated and in distress and so sorry
that I only just now got your message.
Should I come now? Or would you like to
visit for tea? I have something to show
you.
```

3.10 p.m. Oh my God. Oh my God. This is wonderful. Flat is a bit messy. Don't want to put him off and make him think am sluttish housewife. Better go round there. Wonder what he has to show me? – as the actress said to the bishop harrumph, harrumph.

TEN

TOTAL BREAKDOWN

4.30 p.m. My flat. Just back from Mark's house. What just happened?

I waited, nervously, on Mark's doorstep, but this time he opened the door looking different. He was unshaven, in bare feet, wearing jeans and a very dirty dark sweater, and holding an open bottle of red wine. He looked at me strangely.

'Can I come in?' I said eventually. He looked startled by this request.

'Yes, yes, of course, come in.'

He walked through into the kitchen and straight out through the French doors into the garden, breathing in through his nose and appearing to take in the air.

I gasped. The whole place was in bohemian-style chaos. There were piles of washing-up, takeaway cartons, empty wine bottles, lighted candles, and – could that possibly be *joss sticks*?

'What's going on? Why's it all messy? Why hasn't the cleaner been?'

'Given everyone a holiday. Don't need them. Oh!' A wild gleam came into his eye. 'Come and look.'

He started leading me into the living room. 'I've failed at my work,' he said chattily.

'You have?' I said, surveying the once-formal living

room. The floorboards were bare. All the furniture was covered in paint-smeared sheets and there were tins of paint everywhere.

'Yes. Farzad release not happening. Five years' work down the drain. Failed at my life. Failed at my relationships. Failed as a man and a person. But at least I can paint.'

He whipped the sheet off a giant canvas and beamed at me expectantly.

It was absolutely terrible. It looked like the sort of thing you'd buy in Woolworths or from the railings round Hyde Park. There was some sort of sunset and a man galloping through the surf on a horse, a suit of armour abandoned on the beach.

'What do you think?'

I was rescued by my mobile ringing. I looked down – DANIEL FUCKWIT DO NOT ANSWER – and clicked it off quickly.

'Yes, I suppose that's Cleaver, isn't it? Every time I try to do something good, to stick at life, he pops up and ruins it. Honesty, work, trying to do the decent thing – all pointless, isn't it? Charm, and celebrity, that's all it's about. Is he looking after you?'

'No!'

'So he's not supporting you? Is it money you want?'

He went to a jar and starting pulling out £20 notes. 'Here, take it, plenty. Plenty money. Take all you want. Much good it's ever done me.'

'I don't want your money! I'm not some gold-digging single mother coming round to get cash from you. How dare you?' I started heading for the door. 'And, for your information, I'm not with Daniel Cleaver.'

'You're not?'

'No. I'm doing this on my own.'

6.15 p.m. Gaah! Just looked at Daniel's text.

```
DANIEL FUCKWIT DO NOT ANSWER
My darling, darling, darling, etc., etc.
I got your text. Delighted to help, etc.
Working today but will call you later.
Watch Arts Next Week Tonight at 6 p.m. Dx
```

Honestly. Am furious. There is actually a baby involved in this. They did actually both have sex with me and neither of them had a condom. They don't have to both disappear up their own arses.

6.16 p.m. Fumbled grumpily with the TV remotes and eventually found *Arts Next Week Tonight* in the nick of time. There was a studio 'hello' shot of Daniel. He looked raddled, not his usual suave, glowing self, but nevertheless smug and optimistic.

'And now,' said the presenter, 'former publishing executive turned travel-show presenter turned arts-show presenter and a consistent womaniser throughout. Poacher turned gamekeeper – and I mean poacher in the *broadest* sense . . .'

There was stock footage of Daniel with various women, and then a cutaway of Daniel in the studio chair looking, now, completely furious.

'Daniel Cleaver has come out with his attempt at a "serious novel": *The Poetics of Time*. Tom O'Shea! Bill Sharp! Novelists yourselves, and, of course, distinguished critics: Quick thoughts, what do you make of it?'

'This is the single biggest pile of stinking unreadable shit I've ever had the misfortune to plough through,' said Tom O'Shea.

'Bill?'

The two critics were seated beside the presenter, looking very concerned.

'It's neurybathic, neretic, aureate, platitudinous, egregious, insensate, macaronic . . .'

'Could you translate, Bill?' said the presenter.

'Total unreadable toss,' said Bill Sharp.

'Well, let's hear a little bit and decide for ourselves, shall we?' said the presenter.

There was a clip of Daniel in front of a bookshelf, reading earnestly from *The Poetics of Time*:

'The winds shrieked the devil's shroud as the birds cawed beneath Veronica's splayed legs. We gorged, raw. Her eyes were all big.'

There were snorts of laughter from the studio. The show cut to Tom O'Shea and Bill Sharp, helpless with mirth in the studio, and Daniel squirming between them and the presenter.

6.30 p.m. OMG. There is the sound of a key in the lock. Maybe burglars?

'Coo-ey!' My mother. I forgot I gave her a spare key. 'Hello, darling,' said Mum, bustling in with armfuls of carrier bags. 'Well, pop the kettle on!'

Mind started whirring. 'They're electric, they're lethal . . .'

'I was just in Debenhams doing some shopping and I wandered into the maternity department and ta-da!'

She pulled out a giant maternity smock – in the style of the late Princess Diana when she was expecting Prince William and everyone thought you were supposed to conceal your bump instead of spray-tanning it and exposing it on the cover of *Vanity Fair.*

'You see?' she said, holding it up against me. 'You'll look much better in something which covers you up, then you'll look . . .'

'Fat?' I finished for her.

'Well, Mummy has piled on the pounds a bit, hasn't she? Of course I never had that problem. The doctor was telling me to eat Bird's custard and blancmange to put on a bit of flesh.'

'The baby needs to graze.'

'He says, "It's not me who wants the food – it's Mummy!"'

'Mum. Stop. Why do you always make me feel like I've done something wrong? Why are you always trying to change what I wear . . .'

She sank down on the sofa and burst into tears.

'Mum, what's wrong?' I said, putting my arm round her.

'It's just this whole baby business. I mean, of course I

want to be there for you, darling, but if only you could have done it like normal people. It's just thrown everything into disarray. Everything! I just really, really wanted to sit next to the Queen.'

'It's all right, it's all right,' I said, patting her hand. 'But why is it so important to you to sit next to the Queen?'

'It would mean that I meant something if the Queen sat next to me. I've never meant anything. And I've worked really hard for the village all my married life with all the baking and the preserves and everything and it would have meant . . .'

'Like being a hundred or something?'

'Not a HUNDRED, darling!'

'No, I mean like a CBE or a Queen's Guide or something. Like an official stamp of being worthwhile?'

She nodded, wiping her eyes. 'The Admiral says the Queen's table is going to be decided by a vote. I mean, I was hoping you could just sort it out and find out who the father IS – perhaps the baby IS Mark's, and it would be so wonderful for all of us if you were to come to the pre-vote debate and say it was Mark's. Will you? Will you, darling? And will you come to the seating plan event?'

'Mum, I've got an important work meeting tomorrow morning. I need to go to sleep.'

'All right, I must get back to Daddy, anyway. You will come, darling, to the debate?'

'I'll try.'

'. . . and wear the smock?'

Mercifully, the phone rang.

'Better take that, probably work,' I said. 'Bye, Mum.'

She gave me a quick kiss and scuttled out, leaving the smock.

9 p.m. Phone call was from Daniel.

'Christ, Jones, did you see that bloodbath? It was an assassination attempt from the start. Bill Sharp's entire life goal is to prove he's read *The Oxford Dictionary of Incomprehensible Defunct Long Words to Slag People Off With* from cover to cover. As for O'Shea: envy, Jones, the green-eyed monster. They had no understanding of the concept . . .'

By nine-thirty p.m. Daniel was still going on – '. . . this whole baby thing has thrown me off kilter. I could have taken them on if I'd been at the top of my game. *The Poetics of Time* can't be represented by a ten-second sound bite and a couple of resentful goons. It will set the tone, it's all over the wires, and now I have the reviews to face. It's like going over the top, I feel . . .'

There was a texting ping –

MAGDA
Audrona is taking a job designing new
Airbus propeller shafts. I have no nanny.
Help! Can I call you?

This was followed by another text.

TOM
I've just had a blazing row with Shazzer
about the baby thing. She says I AM a horrible person. Am I? Can I call you?

11.20 p.m. Just got off the phone with everyone and a text pinged up from Mark.

MARK DARCY
What did you think of my painting?

MONDAY 20 NOVEMBER

Sit Up Britain **studio.** Sat, exhausted, in the studio control room watching Miranda – immaculate in a cream trouser suit – interviewing the new Minister for Families: for all the world as if she hadn't been shagging the guy she met in Hackney all the previous afternoon and night.

'Listen, Miranda,' the Minister for Families was saying earnestly, 'if we want to give children the best chance in life, the right structures need to be in place: strong and secure traditional families, two confident and able parents, an ethic of responsibility instilled from a young age.'

Something inside me snapped.

'Have you actually been out there in the dating world recently?' I said into Miranda's feed.

'Minister, have you actually been out in the dating world recently?' parroted Miranda.

'Er, well, I have been married for the last fifteen years so . . .'

'Exactly!' I said into the feed. 'It's brutal out there. It's a war! Men are totally self-obsessed and bonkers. Have you any idea how HARD it is to get someone to even TEXT you after you've slept with them . . .'

'Exactly!' began Miranda. 'Men are totally self-obsessed and bonkers. Have you any idea how HARD it is—'

Peri Campos grabbed my mike. 'OK, wrap it up, Bridget's gone mad. Cut to next segment!' as Miranda continued:

'. . . after you've slept with them—'

'I said WRAP IT UP.'

'And, Minister, thank you, we're going to have to leave it there,' said Miranda smoothly. 'And now!' She spun round to look fiercely into Camera 3. 'They're small, they're elliptical killers, and they're ALL OVER YOUR SHOPS.'

News footage flashed across the screen of ambulances, hospitals, people throwing up and chickens.

Miranda looked up at me from the studio chair, holding her hands out, mouthing, 'Where the fuck is it?'

'Jordan!' I hissed. 'The prop!'

Man-bun youth Jordan was turning out to be even worse than Julian. The news clips were on the point of ending as Jordan crawled along the floor and handed the prop to Miranda.

'EGGS!' said Miranda triumphantly, in the nick of time, and held up a small brown egg, which promptly broke in her hand and oozed over her cream suit.

'They're, they're fragile, they're gooey . . .' I ad-libbed desperately.

'They're fragile, they're gooey . . .' parroted Miranda.

'There's one for the Christmas reel,' I continued wildly. 'Jordan. Where the fuck is the egg man?'

'There's one for the Christmas reel. Where the . . .' began Miranda.

'. . . humble egg might seem harmless, if potentially messy' – I free-associated into the feed – 'new findings indicate that the threat of eggs may be . . . Jordan, get him in the chair, get the eggspert in the chair NOW . . . more serious than ever previously . . . OK, he's here! Miranda, go back on script.'

I turned round to see Peri Campos's eyes boring into me.

'You're the one who's elliptical and all over the shop,' she said. 'You were supposed to boil the egg first. I want you in my office, after the show. Cut out of the egg interview. Boring. Drop Nigeria and go to Liz Hurley's bikini line.'

7 p.m. *Sit Up Britain* **loos.** Slumped on the toilet, hand on my bump. None of this is going right. A baby is supposed to bring joy and happiness into the world, but everyone just seems to be falling apart.

7.01 p.m. Must reassure baby that everything is all right. Even though it isn't.

7.02 p.m. It's OK, darling, It's OK, we're going to be OK. I'm sorry about all this mess but you just stay safe and cosy in there and snuggle up and I'll take care of it all and keep you safe.

7.03 p.m. Oh God. It isn't. It really isn't. Texts have started pinging frantically.

MIRANDA
Are we fired?

SHAZZER
Bridge, I've just had a blazing row with
Tom. Can I talk to you?

MAGDA
Bridge — not only do I have no nanny, but
I've just found Jeremy's credit card bill
and it's full of hotels and Agent Provoca-
teur. Will you call me?

MUM
Darling, just wanted to firm up about the
pre-vote debate event. Will you call me?

DANIEL FUCKWIT DO NOT ANSWER
Jones. Could you please call me back? If
it hadn't been for this baby business I
could have defended myself. You have broken me. You owe me some support.

PERI CAMPOS
Bridget: Where the fuck are you? In my office. Now.

7.10 p.m. Think had better call Dad.

ELEVEN

'NO'

7.30 p.m. Still in *Sit Up Britain* toilets. 'Listen, pet,' said Dad on the phone. 'You can't spend your whole time try-ing to please everybody else. You've got a baby to take care of now, and that's what you need to do. One of the best things you can learn in life is how to say no. Or better still, "Absolutely not."'

'But what about—'

'You're exhausted. You need to take care of yourself and your baby. Can you do that if you're going to lis-ten to Daniel going on about his book, sort out Tom's row with Shazzer, sort out Magda's row with her nanny and her husband, come to Mum's Queen visit meeting nightmare? Drive all that way on your own pregnant and have everyone be rude to you, all caught up in their own affairs and asking you difficult questions? And do what-ever ridiculous Peri Campos says?'

'No.'

'Just no?'

'Absolutely not.'

'Exactly. Absolutely not.'

7.45 p.m. Peri Campos's office. Walked in to find Richard Finch sitting, looking mortified, as Peri Campos ranted on: 'She's late, she's disorganised, she spends the whole time in the loo and she's fucking up my show: Bridget Jones!'

'Look, that's not fair,' said Richard. 'Bridget Jones has been the backbone of *Sit Up Britain* for—'

'Zip it, Richard, or you'll be next.'

'Are you going to fire me?' I said.

'No, my love,' she purred. 'I'm not going to fire you. I'm going to get my money's worth out of you. You're going to get in here at eight o'clock every morning. You're going to go through the tabloids, and the gossip mags, you're going to forget about local council election this and Africans with flies in their eyes that, and you're going to come up with some scary, sexy stories that are going to make people actually sit up and either scream or wank but not fall asleep. You cool with that?'

'No,' I said. 'Absolutely not.'

'Bridget, steady on,' said Richard, looking worriedly at my bump.

'*Sit Up Britain* has a long history of serious news reporting,' I said, grandly.

'Yes, I've just been looking at some old footage,' said Peri Campos. 'Was it you I saw climbing up a fireman's pole showing the breathless nation your thong? And parachuting into a sewerage works?'

'Well, the show has always had its – sometimes unintentional – lighter elements,' I conceded.

'And the ratings went off the scale with that thong,' said Richard. 'Bloody nice arse she has.'

'Shut up,' said Peri Campos.

'But *Sit Up Britain* has,' I continued, rather modelling myself on Admiral Darcy, 'throughout its long history, been a bastion of solid national and international news reporting on which our nation relies, and I have no intention of driving myself into a frenzy searching for bits of prurient gossip and bogus media phenomena, and turning perfectly sensible headlines into a baffling attempt at terrifying riddle-me-ree.'

'So does that mean you resign?'

'Yes!' I said. Then immediately panicked.

'Excellent result,' said Peri Campos, while Richard Finch stared at me with a look of pure horror.

'Pruning,' said Peri Campos. 'Pruning is such a great concept because it leads to replenishment.'

'Replenishment? Isn't that a lube?' said Richard.

TUESDAY 21 NOVEMBER

9 p.m. My flat. Just had series of phone calls:

> 'But, darling. I've told everyone you're coming and it'll be absolutely fine. We've brushed over the whole thing in the village and said it was a mistake and . . . please, Bridget, I really need you to be there.'

> 'Come on, Bridge. You've got so boring. You always said you'd never turn into a Smug Mother, and now look at you. You won't be the only one not drinking, what about the alcoholics?'

> 'But, Bridget, you have to have a baby shower: Woney, Mufti, Caroline, Poo . . .'

'But you have to come home for Christmas! You can sleep in the spare room. Una and Geoffrey are coming and . . .'

'But, Jones – you've always been there, in my mind, as my backup position. Nobody takes me seriously. I'm washed up. I need a woman and children to take care of me in my old age. I'm going to be some middle-aged boulevardier, in a cravat, trying to get some sort of affirmation of my sexual viability from the daughters of my friends.'

'No,' I said to all of it, 'absolutely not.'

Twelve

Making the Big from the Small

And then I nested. All through the rest of November, December and January I nested.

I nested all through Christmas. I didn't go anywhere, I didn't buy anything, I just nested and watched TV all Christmas Day and talked on the phone. No Grafton Underwood. No Turkey Curry Buffet. No torture about my romantic life. No, no, absolutely not. It was lovely.

It was so much easier to say no with a baby inside me, because I didn't feel selfish, I felt like I was doing it for him.

MONDAY 15 JANUARY

3 p.m. Dad just came round to take the Magda-gift Bugaboo stroller to put in their garage. 'You'll be better off with a bit more space. When the baby comes, it's just like a little kitten – the stuff is more trouble than the baby. Just put him next to you to sleep and change his nappy and feed him, and that's all you need. How's Mark, by the way?'

'Still crazy. I've told him to stop calling. Daniel the same. Paintings, novels, can't take it.'

Dad said he could help me out with a bit of cash. I said no, because I know they're a bit strapped themselves. It's weird how calm I feel about losing my job. Maybe I'm just baby-stoned, but I have saved up a little bit: not enough to have friezes hand-painted on the walls like Magda, or buy cribs with curtains round, or a bigger flat to fit the Bugaboo stroller in. But I have enough to pay the mortgage for a few months and I don't need much to live on – MASSIVE savings on wine and fags. Also I could always get some work as a freelance journalist or publicist, once I'm feeling a bit better. Or even a telemarketer. I could put on an Indian accent and pretend to be in Mumbai! Or one of those girls who pretends to be an eighteen-year-old busty model and does amusing pornotalk with men online.

And there is so much that needs cleaning and polishing. I mean – unbelievable. Everything I look at needs polishing. Filthy! I literally spent all day today cleaning out cupboards till Dad arrived. It was so satisfying.

And the funny thing is, now that I've shrunk life down to just me and the baby, it's so simple and happy. I don't have to worry about social arrangements or who's fallen out with whom. Every morning I have coffee and a chocolate croissant at Raoul's round the corner, and read *Buddha's Little Instruction Book* and *What to Expect When You're Expecting* and resolve to eat Crossover Foods then go to Pregnancy Yoga and try not to fart. And then I get on with my cupboards and cleaning and have cheesy baked potatoes. And sometimes there's a Dr Rawlings appointment. She thinks I'm doing very well and says, in her personal opinion, fathers can be a terrible nuisance.

*

And, slowly, the friends have all slipped into my routine. Miranda usually comes by with some breakfast on Sundays, on her way back from a club, sometimes with a cute, shag-drunk youth in tow. Tom always comes on Tuesday early evening, because he has a client just near me. And Shazzer comes on Saturday brunch time to rant about whatever the latest outrageous fucking whatever the fuck the fucking thing fucking is.

And Mum has turned her whole campaign round on the basis of inclusivity and got the two gays behind the vicarage on board. Her new thing is to keep dropping into her phone calls, 'So modern to have two fathers – I don't suppose one of them's black, is he, darling?'

And Magda keeps popping round with baby equipment, which is great. She *does* keep saying, though: 'I just think it's going to be really hard doing this on your own down the line, Bridge.' Then she sobs about Jeremy's infidelities. But it's fine, because I realise she doesn't want me to do anything except listen.

Everything's just so good now, because, as Dad says, 'It's coming from the inside, not the outside.'

THIRTEEN

REALISATION

3 p.m. Right. Completely ready for baby now even though not due for seven weeks. Have finished checking packing again. Is as follows:

3 overnight bags containing clothes, toiletries, tennis
    balls, etc.
1 set Scrabble
1 set Boggle
1 pack playing cards
1 portable DVD player
Bag containing 5 hardback books, 8 magazines,
    2 doz. DVDs
1 laptop
1 iPod
1 stopwatch (for timing contractions)
1 bottle Chardonnay (for after birth, obviously)
1 corkscrew
1 box Milk Tray
3 cheesy potatoes
1 bag ice pops (in freezer) to suck on through
    pain

I think that's everything. But it feels like it isn't everything.

9 p.m. Just been reading *Buddha's Little Instruction Book* again:

'If you let cloudy water settle, it will become clear. If you let your upset mind settle, your course will also become clear.'

5 a.m. I miss Mark Darcy.

8 a.m. 'I was waiting for this call,' said Dad. 'Do you love him?'

'More than anyone in the world – I mean apart from the baby, and you, of course.'

'So what's holding you back, pet?'

'Well, first, he's now bonkers, stumbling around doing paintings in the dark; second, he's broken up with me so many times, for reasons I don't understand, that I think if I get back together with him he'll just do it again. I mean, why did he overreact so much at the engagement party and break up our whole lives? Why did he just dump me like that after the christening? Why did he send me that horrible, cold letter after the childbirth class? I'm not intellectual enough for him. Or maybe I'm too old. Never pursue a man, it will only make you unhappy.'

'You girls give men so much power,' said Dad. 'Have you really thought about how he feels? Men have feelings too, they just don't go on about them all the time. You have to be nurturing of the other person's self-esteem. Talk to him. You can't just sit around waiting to be rescued.'

'But why did he keep leaving like that? Why has he gone mad?'

'You'll have to work that out for yourself, love. But I've known Mark since he was a little boy. I used to watch him, packed off to the station in his little suit and stiff collar, carrying his little suitcase. Then, when he was a teenager, he was always the quiet, spotty one in the geeky sweater in the corner: the best of all the lads, but never the one who got the girl. You'll know when you know. You'll see.'

10 p.m. Feel like scales are falling from my eyes. Well, not literally scales. Not weighing scales. But realise I've been seeing men as all-powerful gods with the gift to decide whether I'm worthy or attractive or not, instead of human beings. I have not been thinking about what they feel. I have to . . . I have to . . . oh, I'm so sleepy.

SATURDAY 3 FEBRUARY

5 a.m. My flat. I understand, I do, I think. It's what Daniel represents.

5 a.m. My flat. But then I still think it was bloody brutal to send me that letter. I mean, it wasn't me that acted out in the childbirth class, it was Daniel. Why take it out on me? Blurry bastard.

5 a.m. My flat. I just daren't call him. I daren't. It'll hurt too much if he says no.

1 p.m. My flat. Gaah! It's one in the afternoon. I'm starving, the baby's starving. Have to get up and get some food.

1.05 p.m. Gaah! What's that?

1.06 p.m. Is baby in stomach. Has started to feel like giant frozen turkey.

1.10 p.m. Cannot put socks on, baby is so enormous.

1.30 p.m. Oh God. There's no food in the fridge. I have no cash. I'm starving. The baby's starving.

1.31 p.m. I'll just have a little lie-down.

1.55 p.m. Just spent ten minutes trying to get up from sofa as had got hands stuck under stomach. Magda is right, cannot do anything on my own. Cannot call Mark to help after all this time, as will seem like act of desperation, not because I really love and understand him. Have to manage by myself, pull self together and go out and forage for food.

3 p.m. Tesco Metro. 'Is it a boy or a girl?' asked a shopper as I tried to reach the cheesy potatoes.

'Boy!'

'When's it due?'

'March!' I said. Realised, now with my pregnancy public, I had started to feel not so much like Her Majesty the Queen, but like an air hostess, only with human head attached to elephant's body, saying same thing to one person after another with fixed grin.

'When's it due?'

'March. Thank you for flying with us,' I said, distractedly.

'Is it a boy or a girl?' said the cashier as she rang up my shopping and I fumbled to get my credit card out of my purse.

'Boy, two years' time. It's an elephant,' I said, sliding my card into the machine and adding, 'Can I have fifty pounds cash back, please?'

'Just enter your PIN.'

I stared blankly at the cashier.

'Just pop your PIN in here.'

People in the queue behind me were starting to mutter things.

'Pregnant women! Forget everything!'

'I think it's a girl, she's carrying lopsided.'

'Do you think she's all right?'

'Look,' said the cashier. 'Get on with it.'

'I can't remember my PIN.'

Started jabbing different numbers frantically. My birthday? Nope. My actual weight and my ideal weight? Nope. The baby had eaten the part of my brain with the PIN in it.

'She's firing blanks,' said the man behind me.

Firing blanks. Firing blanks.

'Have you got another card?'

'No,' I said, fumbling in my wallet for cash: nothing but a 50p coin. 'Don't suppose you do credit?' I gabbled. 'I'm a regular customer. I'm very trustworthy. I used to work for the TV – *Sit Up Britain*?'

'Sorry.'

I shouldn't have told her it was an elephant.

Firing blanks. That's what Daniel said to Mark after the childbirthing class, when Mark was so angry and I went off in the taxi. Suddenly remembered looking back at the two of them, through the taxi's rear window. I saw Daniel saying something intently to Mark, then Mark stormed off. Something happened. It was after that conversation, the same night, when Mark sent me the letter.

I took out my phone, right there in Tesco Metro, and dialled.

'Daniel?'

'Yes, Jones. I'm about to do an interview about *The Poetics of Time* for the most important arts programme in Monaco. But what may I help you with?'

'You know after the childbirthing class?'

'I do know after it, yes, Jones.'

'What did you say to Mark?'

There was silence on the other end.

'Daniel?' I said dangerously.

'Yes, I was meaning to call you about that, Jones. I may have implied to Darce that, when you and I had our delightful thrust towards conception, I did not, as it were, *dress for the occasion* . . .'

'You WHAT? But you did wear a condom. You lied! You absolute bastard!'

'Come on, Jones. It's only Darcy. Oops. Got to go, Monte Carlo on the line. *Bonjour, les petites Monacaines!* Bye, Jones.'

That's it! That's it, I thought, standing by the tills in Tesco Metro as people bustled by, tutting, with their shopping. Mark is a man of honour and he thought that I had lied. On top of everything else, he thought I'd lied to him about the condoms. I have to call him immediately. Anything could happen. He could remarry Natasha. He could go back to the Maghreb and never return. He could have become a successful painter and at this moment be chatting up a gallery owner wearing a weird outfit and hat in Shoreditch.

3.30 p.m. Oh shit. Oh shit! iPhone has turned itself off. Cannot remember iPhone password.

3.45 p.m. Back in flat. OK. Calm and poised. I will let my upset mind settle like a glass of mud and . . . What the fuck is the password?

3.46 p.m. The baby's due date? 1703? 0317? Nope. Also was not even having baby when put password in phone. OK: when I was thirty-two Mark was . . . no. When I am sixty-five Daniel will be . . . still a fuckwit. Oh God, oh God. I have to get hold of him.

3.47 p.m. I know! Will call Mark from good old-fashioned landline.

3.48 p.m. Oh. What is Mark's phone number?

4 p.m. Maybe is in phone book on the computer.

4.05 p.m. Computer screen said: ENTER PASSWORD.

4.15 p.m. Baby? Mark. MarkDaniel? Cheese? Potato? Cheesy potato?

4.30 p.m. The baby has eaten every number in my head. Cannot remember Shazzer's number, or Tom's number, or Dad's number. I have no cash. I have no brain.

5 p.m. Staring blankly at wall. Is not baby's fault. Is technology.

5.30 p.m. Grrr! Hate technology. Wish technology had never been invented. When did it suddenly happen that you can't do anything without remembering some sort of weird mixed-up name or number? Is exactly like car burglar alarms used to be when your car was more likely to be broken into if you *had* a car alarm because the alarm kept going off and annoying everyone so much that they simply smashed the window and broke it. Passwords are supposed to stop Russian hackers from getting into the computer – not stop YOU from getting into your own computer, or indeed anything, while the Russian hackers get on with hacking all your stuff.

*

6.30 p.m. Please, my child. Give forth thy passwords back to what is left of my brain, so that I might tell Mark that we love him and want him to be thy father, and – crucially – bring forth a cheesy potato that I might nourish thee.

Then suddenly, miraculously, it came to me:

5287

I checked the numbers and letters on the landline phone.

5287

J A U R

JUST AS U R

6.45 p.m. Lunged at the mobile and found Mark's number in Contacts. Hands shaking, I called him. I got his voicemail.

'Mark, it's Bridget. I have something very, very important

to say to you. I did not lie to you about the condoms. It was Daniel who lied. It's you I love. I love you. Please call me. Please call me.'

6.46 p.m. Nothing. Maybe Mark has forgotten *his* password.

7 p.m. Just texted Mark the same message. Maybe he's still painting. Maybe I should go round there. Oh God. I have to get some phone, I mean food. Maybe I'll get some cash first, so nothing else can go wrong.

Limped, broken, downstairs to the cash machine booth at the bank. Went through the automatic doors, put my handbag down and entered the PIN. It didn't work. Why didn't it work? Maybe I'd entered it too many times. Stumbling, as if in a dream, I went back out to the street, through the automatic doors, then suddenly, just as they closed, saw that my bag was still on the floor inside.

Oh God, oh God. My phone was in the bag, as well as my wallet and the keys to my flat.

And the doors to the bank wouldn't open.

8.30 p.m. Slumped on doorstep outside my flat. Whole idea of making the big small is just bollox. Magda is right.

8.35 p.m. It has started to rain: really lots and lots of rain.

8.40 p.m. Maybe I could ask a kindly stranger to lend me their phone? But then, what is the point if cannot remember anyone's phone numbers? Still, maybe through a dream state . . . there is a man approaching!

I started to say, 'Excuse me?' – but he just dropped a coin on my coat and hurried off, looking frightened. Obviously thinks am desperate pregnant baby lady, like Thomas Hardy's Fanny Robin dying in the snow.

Hearing footsteps, I raised my head wearily, perhaps for the last time, and saw, once again, a familiar figure in a dark blue overcoat, striding towards me through the rainy street.

Fourteen

Reconciliation

'What are you doing sitting in the rain?' said Mark, hurrying towards me. He helped me up, and started taking off his overcoat. 'I just missed your call. I was in court.'

'In court? What about your painting?'

'Terrible rubbish. Don't mention it again, I've been calling you constantly since you rang.'

'My phone's in my bag stuck in the bank.'

'Your bag's stuck in the bank? Here, put this on.'

He put his overcoat on my shoulders.

'Why are you on the doorstep? Where are your keys?'

'They're in the bag in the bank.'

'They're in the bag in the bank. Jolly good. Won't enquire further right now. So! Business as usual.'

He rattled the door a few times and tried to slip the lock with his credit card.

'OK,' he said, 'probably get barred from the Bar for this, but here we go.'

He smashed the side window with his fist and opened the door from the inside.

I started my speech on the way up the stairs.

'I'm so happy to see you. I didn't lie to you. I'd never lie to you. There were dolphin condoms both times. I realised I've been brainwashed over the years by all the things that have happened, and dating self-help books and all the dating advice and to think that a way to a man's heart is to seem not very interested in him. That you mustn't let a man know you fancy him in case he thinks you fancy him and . . .'

Of course the door to the actual flat was locked as well. Mark took out his credit card and simply slipped the lock.

'Yes, I think we need to look at some security issues here. You were saying?'

'I thought that you mustn't let an old love know you still love him, in case he thinks you still love him.'

He went completely silent and still.

'Mark?'

'Yes?'

'I love you.'

'You love me?'

'Yes. And I'm really, simply, genuinely sorry.'

'No, *I'm* sorry.'

'No, *I'm* sorry.'

'But it was no more your fault than mine,' he said.

'No. It was my fault. Now I'm *having* a child, I realise – on that occasion and many other occasions – I didn't need to react like a child.'

'Well, it wasn't exactly like a child,' he said.

'Good point. Pretty drunk for a child.'

'That would be actually pretty alarming.' He smiled and picked up a bottle of wine. 'Is this for the baby?'

'Mark, what I'm trying to say is I'm sorry that I hurt y—'

'But this has no logic, I hurt you too. We must both apo—'

'Look. Can I make the speech, please?' I said.

'Yes.'

'I'm sorry.'

'We've had that.'

'Mark, stop it. Listen. Stop being a barrister, stop being an alpha male, just be a person.'

He looked confused for a second, like his whole sense of self was collapsing again.

'It's you I love,' I said. 'Whatever happens, whatever you decide to do, it will always be you. I've lived quite a long time now. Of all the people I've met in the world in my quite long life, you are the most decent, the kindest, the most intelligent, the most sensitive, with the deepest soul.' I noticed he was looking slightly disappointed. 'And also,' I added hurriedly, 'the hottest, the most handsome, witty and charming.' He was starting to look really pleased now. 'The most stylish! And the best, most amazing shag ever.' He was positively beaming. 'You are the person I most love in all the world,' I went on, 'apart from the baby, and it's you that I really want from the depths of my heart to be the father to this baby.'

I thought for a second. 'I mean, obviously, Shaz, Tom and Miranda say you have a poker up your arse and are anally retentive and avoidant, and you're always talking about work, and always on the phone and—'

'PERMANENTLY on the phone, stuck up, and snobbish, and emotionally stunted,' Mark added, sheepishly.

'But they're completely wrong. The truth is I love you very much . . .'

'. . . with a few adjustments perhaps: Wittier? More spontaneous? More playful? More charming? More . . . ?'

'No,' I said. 'Just as you are.'

'That's my line.'

The smoke alarm went off.

'Shit, the curry.'

'You've made CURRY?' said Mark, genuinely frightened now. 'Happy Valentine's Day, by the way.'

'No, it's takeaway from the Pink Elephant. It's VALENTINE'S DAY? I forgot I put it in the oven the day before yesterday to heat up,' I yelled over the noise of the smoke alarm.

Acrid fumes were belching from the oven.

Mark miraculously remembered and punched in the alarm code, saying, 'Yes, Valentine's Day,' turned on the extractor fan and opened the French windows. Once the alarm had stopped, he opened the oven. He pulled out a melted polystyrene carton with the curry in it.

'Do you know one of the things I love most about you, Bridget?'

'What?' I said excitedly, thinking I was about to be praised: for being intelligent or pretty.

'That in all the time I've known you I've never once been bored by you.'

'Oh,' I said, wondering if being not boring was good? I mean, on the scale of things people might love you for?

'There have been several near-death experiences, I've been on fire – both sexually in your bed and physically in your kitchen, I've been poisoned, I've been crazed

184

with lust, furious, heartbroken, humiliated, embarrassed, ecstatic, soaked, covered in cake, confounded by your idiosyncratic, though largely valid, internal logic, insulted by drunks, forced into breaking-and-entering scenarios, fights, in legal extremis, Third World jail, embarrassing parental occasions, vomit, professional humiliation, but never for a single second have I been bored.'

He noticed my expression.

'But am I intelligent?' I said.

'Very, *very* intelligent. Intellectual giant.'

'And pretty and thin?' I said hopefully.

'Very, very pretty and very thin – apart from being completely spherical: spherical yet brave. You've been absolutely heroic and magnificent the last eight months, doing this on your own with all these antics in the background. And now you're going to do it with me, whoever's biological baby it is. I love you and I love our baby.'

'I love you both too,' I said ecstatically.

It was the best Valentine's Day ever. Later that night, we ordered Chinese takeaway and ate it in front of the fire (the fire in the fireplace). And we talked and we talked and we talked and we talked about everything that had happened, and why. And we made plans for how it was going to be. We decided to stay in my flat, just for now, so as not to cause a rumpus.

'It's cosy,' said Mark. 'And I like the cooking.'

It turned out Mark had heard about the *Sit Up Britain* debacle from Jeremy, and he'd talked to Richard Finch and Peri Campos. He said what they'd done was technically lawful, but – as Peri Campos eventually conceded – not ethical and he told me what I needed to do to get the job back and maternity leave.

And it felt very easy and simple and just like this was how it was supposed to be. It felt like coming home. And then we went to bed. And it was, Miranda would say, *A. May. Zing.*

'Pregnant women don't shag like that,' said Mark.

'Oh yes they fucking well do.'

FIFTEEN

HER MAJESTY SAVES THE DAY, SORT OF

2 p.m. Grafton Underwood village hall. Result of the Grafton Underwood voting as to who would sit next to the Queen during the Queen's luncheon on the other side from the vicar.

Mark and I entered the village hall, via separate doors, somewhat furtively, so as not to draw attention. Mum was taking the microphone on the stage.

'Lord Mayor, Lord Clerk to Her Majesty,' began Mum, in a nervous, querulous voice, quite unlike her usual airy, bossy tone.

'Objection!' Mavis Enderbury leapt to her feet. 'That should be Clerk, not Lord Clerk.'

'Oh my godfathers, I'm so sorry.' Mum was seriously losing it. 'Anyway, here is our very own master and commander of the seas, and captain of the plucky ship of Grafton Underwood: Admiral Darcy!' said Mum, then slunk back to her seat, looking shaken.

Mark's father, tall, still handsome in his admiral's outfit, strode onto the stage.

'Right! Let's get on. Seating plan,' he boomed. 'I am happy to announce that to Her Majesty's left will be, of course, the vicar, and to her right, as the result of our vote . . .'

There were ripples all over the hall as the Admiral took

out an envelope stamped with an old-fashioned dark red wax seal.

'To Her Majesty's right,' his face broke into a fond smile, 'a woman who has worked tirelessly her entire life for this village . . . and whose Salmon à la King has kept us nourished for decades: Mrs Pamela Jones.'

'Objection!' Mavis Enderbury leapt again to her feet, face twisted angrily beneath a hat-like hairdo.

'Could we all please think for a moment, not of ourselves, but of our Leader of Church and State – Her Royal Majesty?' said Mavis. 'In our chosen Village Representative – who will be engaging Her Majesty's right, and in royal banter – do we want a representative of our decency and family values? Or the adulterous mother of an unmarried, pregnant daughter, who doesn't know who the father is and one of them might be black?'

There was uproar as Mavis looked straight at me, prompting everyone to stare. Mark was heading for the microphone, but the village was already speaking for itself.

'Shame on you, Mavis,' roared Uncle Geoffrey. 'Racist and rubbish, and Bridget is a lovely girl with lovely big—'

'Geoffrey!' said Auntie Una.

'Look at Joanna Lumley,' said Dad, leaping to his feet.

Everyone fell reverentially silent.

'Joanna Lumley was a single mother and wouldn't tell anyone who the father was for years.'

'Good point, excellent woman,' said Penny Husbands-Bosworth.

'Quite so. Military family,' said Admiral Darcy.

'The Virgin Mary didn't know who the father was!' said Mum, hopefully.

'Yes, she did!' said the vicar. 'It was God.'

'Yes, but I bet everyone in the village was saying it was the Angel Gabriel,' said Dad.

'Or Jesus,' I added helpfully.

'Jesus was the *baby*,' yelled Mavis Enderbury.

'The point is people gossip,' said Dad, gently but firmly. 'And gossip isn't right.'

Mark leapt onto the stage, in full barrister mode.

'Mr Colin Jones has hit the nail on the head,' he thundered. 'We live in a country – a country once renowned for its values – which increasingly is run by the village gossips, in the form of some aspects of the press. But here, in this village hall, with your clear rejection of a small attempt at spite, we see what it once meant, and still must mean, to be British.'

There was the noise of general, if slightly unclear why, self-congratulation.

'Look at Her Majesty herself,' continued Mark.

Everyone sat up excitedly, like meerkats.

'Look at the tabloid drubbing she endured when her family was mired in confusion and infidelity. Look how she has soldiered on, still loving her family: loyal, decent, dutiful but elastic, as all families and communities must be. We are all distracted by the glamour and shine of the evolving world. But we must stay rooted in who we are: in strength, decency, resilience, yes, but not in judgement. And I say this to you now, as, not only a son of this village, but' – he looked across at me and smiled – 'as the father—'

There were ripples all over the hall.

'Yes, yes – whoever the biological father turns out to be, and we don't know yet – the *father* of Grafton Underwood's about to be newest grandchild.'

Everyone cheered.

'Ladies and gentlemen,' said the Admiral, visibly moved but holding it together. 'It may be unconstitutional: but let's take another vote. All those in favour of Pamela Jones sitting to Her Majesty's right during the post-ceremony luncheon?'

Everyone raised his or her hand, including Mavis.

'Motion carried. Pamela Jones will sit to Her Majesty's right.'

There was applause and cheers. Then, quite suddenly, Admiral Darcy turned to Mark and *hugged* him.

'I say, steady on,' said Uncle Geoffrey.

The old Admiral struggled with himself.

'I love you, son,' he said. 'I always did.'

'I love you too, Father.'

'Anyway. Jolly good. Let's press on.'

As Mark said in the car, when we finally escaped all the tears and hugging, 'The whole thing was so ludicrous that it was really hard for anyone to keep any sort of tenuous grip on reality.'

But it's nice to have that shared history. And, you see, Billy, this is why it means so much to me that you remember what Mark said that day. The world you're about to enter will be a different sea, with so much to do with how many likes you get on Facebook or who knows what; where everyone is showing off rather than sharing their sadnesses and fears and what they really feel; and 'liking' the most famous, or the richest, or the prettiest, more than the most human, or the kindest friend. You are the Grafton Underwood New Generation. And before you know it, Mark and me will be throwing Turkey Curry Buffets, Brunch Time Karaoke and trying to set you up with Una Alconbury's granddaughter.

Sixteen

Phantom Pregnancy

Friday 16 March

7 a.m. My flat. Baby is due tomorrow. Am so excited.

Saturday 17 March

9 p.m. My flat. Baby still has not come.

Monday 19 March

Babies: 0

Wednesday 21 March

5 p.m. My flat. Baby *still* has not come. Feel like toddler sent to sit on potty and failing to produce poo, while adults wait, increasingly frostily, outside bathroom door. Maybe I actually am an elephant. Maybe it's going to take two years.

Thursday 22 March

4 p.m. My flat. Baby has not come. Is getting really uncomfortable now: like having a frozen ostrich inside me.

Maybe he's suddenly just going to *burst out* like the Alien and eat his way through my stomach and loom out as a fully formed toddler asking for his iPad and yelling, 'I just want to finish this levellllllll!'

7 a.m. My flat. 'We can always go get a curry?' I said hopefully to Mark, as he prepared to leave for work.

'Nooo! Not curry. I'm scarred for life by burning foam and curry. Why don't you just get a bit more . . . ready?'

8 a.m. OK. Will check packing again. Maybe I need a fifth bag, just a small holdall for— Ooh, telephone!

'Oh, darling, I'm so excited. The Queen is going to be here this afternoon. I can't believe it's actually happening. Any sign? You know, I was thinking about you and Mark mentioning "William" for the name; it's a bit samey, isn't it? What about Maddox? You know Shiloh is Heaven spelt backwards. Isn't that super?'

'Super,' I said, dully, writing SHILOH on a Post-it note. 'No, it isn't. It's Holish.'

'Don't be silly, darling. It's not Polish. Have you tried that cod liver oil yet? Ooh, must run! The Lord Lieutenant's here! Bridget! I'm going to actually sit next to the Queen!'

Suddenly felt I was going to cry. All those months of working and now Mum's dream – however bonkers – had come true. 'Good luck, Mum. Enjoy it. You've earned it. Charm the pants off her.'

9 a.m. Baby still has not come. Feel somehow fraudulent. Maybe it is a phantom pregnancy and the whole thing . . . Oh, goody! Phone again!

Was Magda with oddly cold tone.

'I suppose Miranda and Shazzer were the first to hear, even though it's me that's supported you all the way through, but Miranda and Shazzer are more fun and exciting, aren't they?'

'What do you mean?'

'The baby. You might have told me, after everything I've done.'

'The baby hasn't come,' I said.

'OH! I thought you'd crossed me off the list. But, Bridget, you're a week late! You're going to be split in two. You need to get it induced.'

'What list?'

'You have made a birth announcement list? You need to get it ready in your email. You won't be able to pull up all those email addresses when you're postpartum.'

10 a.m. Magda is right. I don't want to be *pulling up addresses* and deciding what to say, when am in middle of newborn baby joy.

10.05 a.m. If alleged baby actually exists.

Noon. Right. Have pretty much got everyone's addresses assembled now.

```
Mark and Bridget are pleased to an-
nounce . . .
```

12.15 p.m. Hmm, though. We've been keeping it low-key amongst the friends about being together till the paternity is resolved so as not to hurt Daniel's feelings.
   12.30 p.m.

```
Bridget is pleased to welcome into the
world . . .
```

– Yuk, creepy.

12.45 p.m.

```
Ladies and gentlemen. Please welcome . . .
```

Nope. Sounds like an MC at the Royal Variety Show. How about something more upbeat?

1 p.m.

```
Sender: Bridget Jones
Subject: Baby!
It's a boy! Bridget Jones has given
birth to a baby boy, William Harry,
7lb, 8oz. Both mother and baby are doing
well.
```

1.15 p.m. Sounds a bit 'samey'.

PS Bridget died in childbirth.

1.16 p.m. Heeheehee. OK, SAVE.

1.17 p.m. Oh my God. Oh my God. Have pressed SEND ALL.

3 p.m. Total disaster. Both phones are going mental, ringing off the hook and texts keep pinging up every four seconds. Just opened email box: twenty-six emails.

'Congratulations!'

'The dying bit was a joke, right?'

3.10 p.m. Gaah! Doorbell.

3.16 p.m. It's a giant bunch of flowers from *Sit Up Britain*.

Gaah! Doorbell again.

3.30 p.m. It's a giant fluffy bunny from Miranda with a note saying, 'It's cute, it's fluffy and I'm going to boil it!'

OK. OK. Calm, calm. Will simply send another group email and put it all right.

And maybe send back the flowers with a note of apology. And the bunny. Though it is really cute and does not deserve to be boiled.

3.35 p.m. God, wish the phone would stop ringing and pinging, right.

    Sender: Bridget Jones
    Subject: Ignore last email.
    Dear all, I'm really sorry, but I haven't
    actually had the baby yet. But when I do

have the baby I'll be sure to let you know
when that happy time comes!

3.45 p.m. Have sent it.

3.46 p.m. Oh, though. How can I now then send them another email when the baby actually does come? I'm like the boy who cried wolf. No one will believe me.

SEVENTEEN

THE ARRIVAL

6 p.m. My flat. Yayy! Mark is back from work.

'God, those stairs,' he said, letting himself in, tie loosened, shirt slightly undone, all post-work and horny-looking. 'Sorry I'm late, darling,' he said, kissing me on the lips. 'The whole city's gridlocked. Had to abandon the car, and take the tube. Where's this email you're so upset about?'

Sheepishly, I showed him the email disaster.

I love the way he just looks really quickly at something – something which totally freaks me out and bothers me for days – and, as if he's at work, makes a very quick assessment of how important it is, and how much time it deserves, and just deals with it.

'OK. It's just extremely amusing,' he said. 'You've corrected the error. Don't give it any more thought. What are all these bags?'

'My packing!' I said proudly.

'Right,' said Mark. 'I was thinking, now that you're overdue and with the stairs and everything, maybe we should cut it down a little?'

'Owwwwwwwwwwwwwwwwwwww!' Suddenly the worst cramp/spasm/pain I'd ever felt in my life invaded me. 'Owwwwwwwwwwwwwwwwwwwwwwwwwwwwwwww-wwwww!'

'Right, um, jolly good. Ah. I sent my car and driver away. Your car?'

'I left it at Magda's,' I said, panicked.

'Bridget. Stop panicking. I'll call Addison Lee. You have to be calm or—'

'Owwwwwwwwww!'

'Oh, my God, oh my God,' gabbled Mark. 'It's only two minutes since the last contraction. You're going to give birth in the car!'

'Stop panicking. Owww!'

Mark's phone rang. He looked at it intensely.

'Bloody work!' he suddenly yelled, and threw it out of the window.

'Noooooooo!' I yelled, watching the phone about to hurtle down three storeys.

We looked at each other, wild-eyed.

'Use my phone,' I said.

'OK, OK,' said Mark. 'Where is it?'

'I don't know!'

'Put your feet up, breathe.' He found the phone, groaned when he got voicemail and put it on speaker-phone.

'All our customer service specialists are currently on other calls, as we are currently experiencing heavy delays owing to increased demand.'

'Ambulance?' He dialled 999. 'I see, very well. City's gridlocked,' he said, clicking off the phone, just as I was hit by another contraction. 'Emergencies only. Apparently, normal childbirth isn't an emergency.'

'Not an emergency?' I yelled. 'I feel like I'm about to

push an ostrich out of my body. Fuck! Can you get the ice pops out of the freezer?'

'I'm going to text everyone,' said Mark, fumbling in the freezer. 'Someone has to be in the area.'

'Let's get down in the street and see if we can hail a cab,' I said.

'Do we really need all this stuff?'

'Yes! Yes. I have to have tennis balls and the ice pops.'

Mark half dragged, half carried me to the main road and then went back for the four bags. The traffic really was solid: unmoving, buses, lorries, honking and belching fumes. By some virgin-birth-style miracle, a taxi rounded a side street with its light on. Mark practically threw himself on the bonnet.

'Going somewhere nice?' said the driver, as Mark loaded the bags into the cab. 'Owwww!' I yelled, at which the driver looked terrified. ''Ere you're not goner give birth in me cab, are you?'

'Suck on this,' said Mark, handing me an ice pop. 'The Queen, by the way, has just arrived at Grafton Underwood village hall.'

'This isn't an ice pop,' I said. 'It's a frozen sausage!'

After twenty minutes of the driver going on and on about just having had his cab cleaned, we'd gone only a quarter of a mile and the contractions were coming every thirty seconds.

'Right. This is hopeless. We're going to have to walk,' said Mark.

'Great, excellent idea, sir, if I may say so, out you get,' said the cabbie, manhandling me out of his cab.

'What about my packing?' I wailed.

'Sod the packing,' said Mark, hauling the four bags into a newsagent's and handing the baffled newsagent twenty quid.

'I'm going to have to carry you!'

He picked me up, like Richard Gere in *An Officer and a Gentleman*, and then stumbled under the weight. 'Oh Christ Alive, you're enormous.'

The phone rang. 'Hang on, let me put you down a sec. Cleaver! – Cleaver's running from his flat – yes! I'm carrying her! We're just at the junction of Newcomen Street and the A3.'

We staggered along the street, both groaning, Mark frequently putting me down and clutching his back.

Then Daniel appeared, red-faced, jogging and panting.

'Cleaver,' said Mark, 'this is probably the only time in my life I've actually been pleased to see you.'

'Right. Everyone relax. I'll take charge. I'll take the head, you take the feet,' said Daniel, wheezing as if he was about to have a heart attack.

'No, I'll take the head,' said Mark.

'Nope. I started this off and—'

'Will you please. Stop. Squabbliiiiiiiiiiiiiiiiing,' I said, and bit hard into Mark's hand, at which they both let go of my arms and only just caught me.

It ended up with the three of us staggering like some

weird push-me-pull-you to A&E and getting stuck in the revolving door.

Finally we managed to get out of the door and into the hospital. Daniel and Mark staggered to the reception desk, holding me between them like a sack of cheesy potatoes, and dumped me on the reception desk.

'Who's the father?' said the receptionist.

'I'm the father,' said Daniel.

'No, *I'm* the father,' said Mark, just as Dr Rawlings burst through the doors, pushing a trolley.

'They're both the fathers,' said Dr Rawlings, as the three of them manhandled me onto the trolley.

This is not, I thought, not for the first time in this sorry saga, how I imagined this moment would be.

EIGHTEEN

YOU MADE IT!

9 p.m. Hospital delivery room. 'There you are, one absolutely perfect, beautiful, baby boy.'

Dr Rawlings handed you to me, and I actually saw her wipe away a tear. 'I never thought I'd see the day,' she said in a choked voice.

And there you were, in my arms, your skin next to my skin, not a little turkey in my stomach but a little person. You were waving your miniature fists, trying to speak to me: tiny, perfect, entirely beautiful. You looked straight into my eyes, and, I don't suppose you remember, but the first thing we ever did was rub noses.

'Hello, darling,' I said through my tears. 'Hello, my darling. I'm your mum. We made it through.'

Looked up at Mark and Daniel to see that both of them were in tears too.

'It's just, it's all been so emotional,' sobbed Daniel, clutching Mark's arm.

'I know, I know,' Mark managed to get out. 'Look, can you let go?'

'Oh, for heaven's sake, pull yourselves together,' said Dr Rawlings. 'Never heard such a bloody drama.'

The door burst open.

'Bridget!' said Mum, pushing everyone aside to be first. 'Do you know, I had just sat down next to Her Majesty when I got the call? I came straight away. I mean, obviously, some things are more important than the Queen, but then—'

'Pamela,' said Dad. 'Look. Your grandson.'

'Oh,' she said. 'Oh my darling. My little boy.'

I gently handed you to her and her face crumpled. 'Oh Bridget. He's perfect.'

It was the sweetest thing. Then she said: 'Could we text a picture of this to the Queen?'

Miranda burst in with a bottle of mojito mix, followed by a beaming Richard Finch. 'Bridget Jones. I'm so proud of you.' He peered at me, worried for a second. 'Oh, thank God, the giant boobs are still there.'

Everyone turned up. Tom and Shazzer were hugging each other and everyone in sight. Jeremy got all sentimental with Magda, putting his arm round her. 'I'm so sorry, my love. It's all going to be different now. All our babies. All those years.'

'You are still. In. The. Doghouse,' said Magda.

Just then the doors flung open again and Mark and Daniel appeared, looking nervous.

Everyone looked at them. 'So?'

'We have to wait,' said Mark. Daniel reached out for Mark's hand. Mark didn't protest, and the two of them sat, holding hands.

'And the winner is!' said Dr Rawlings, bursting through the doors. 'Can I announce it in front of everyone or do you want to be alone? It's rather fun, isn't it? – like the final of *The X Factor.*'

'I think we're all family, aren't we?' I said to Mark and Daniel. They both nodded nervously.

'All right, then. The father of Bridget Jones's baby is none other than . . .'

And Finally . . .

'Mark Darcy!'

'Oh, thank Christ for that,' said Daniel as I handed you to your real daddy. 'I mean, don't take it the wrong way, Jones,' he added hurriedly, seeing my face. 'Adorable, charming obviously. I just know my limitations. May the best man win!'

Mark was looking at you, bursting with love and pride. 'Why don't you ask?' he whispered.

'Daniel,' I said. 'Would you like to be his godfather?'

'Well, that's um, absolutely . . .' For a moment Daniel choked up, then he pulled himself together. 'That's a brave and big-hearted offer. Yes, thank you,' said Daniel. 'And since my godchild is a boy, you don't have to worry about me trying to shag her when she's twenty.'

'Right. That's quite enough. Let's all leave the room,' said Dr Rawlings. 'And let Mum and . . . Dad . . . finally have some time alone with their son.'

'Dr Rawlings,' said Daniel, as everyone made their way out. 'May I say that I have never in my life seen anyone look quite so sexual in a white coat.'

'Oh, you are such a naughty man,' she said, and giggled.

*

'Wait,' I said, as my dad was leaving. 'You haven't held him yet.'

Dad, or Grandad now, touched your cheek very gently.

'Oops, better not let his head fall off,' said Dad as Mark very awkwardly and nervously handed you over. Then Dad (my dad) looked down into your eyes, his little grandson's eyes.

'Take care of him,' he said, throatily, to Mark. 'And of her.'

'Mr Jones. If I am a fraction as good a father as you have been to Bridget, then I will be—'

'*He* will be the luckiest baby in the world,' said Dad.

Just then your little fist flailed, hit a switch on the monitor, and knocked a glass of blackcurrant cordial over, which smashed, spilling blackcurrant everywhere. Lights flashed and the machine started emitting an urgent blaring noise as if there was about to be an airborne attack.

Dr Rawlings rushed back into the delivery room, looking panicked, followed by everyone else.

'Like mother, like son,' bellowed Mark above the din. 'Bridget?'

'What?' I yelled.

'Will you marry me?'

'Jones?' yelled Daniel, with a conspiratorial glance at Mark. 'I suppose one last shag would be out of the question?'

'Yes!' I shouted, in joyful, wonderful, overwhelmed reply to both of them.

* * *

And that, my little darling, is how I came to be your mum.

Acknowledgements

Gillon Aitken, Clare Alexander, Sunetra Atkinson, Helen Atkinson-Wood, María Benitez, Grazina Bilunskiene, Helena Bonham Carter, Charlotte and Alain de Botton, Richard Cable, Susan Campos, Liza Chasin, Richard Coles, Rachel Cugnoni, Dash and Romy Curran, Kevin Curran, Richard Curtis, Scarlett Curtis, Patrick Dempsey, Paul Feig, Eric Fellner, the Fielding Family, Colin Firth, Carrie Fisher, Piers and Paula Fletcher, Stephen Frears, Jules Gishen, Amelia Granger, Hugh Grant, Simon Green, Debra Hayward, Susanna Hoffs, Jimmy Horowitz, Jenny Jackson, Simon Kelner, Charlie Leadbeater, Tracey MacLeod, Marianne Maddalene, Sharon Maguire, Murillo Martins, Karon Maskill, Dan Mazer, Sonny Mehta, Maile Meloy, Leah Middleton, Abi Morgan, David Nicholls, Catherine Olim, Imogen Pelham, Sally Riley, Renata Rokicki, Mike Rudell, Darryl Samaraweera, Tim Samuels, Emma Thompson, Patricia Toro Quintero, Daniel Wood, Renée Zellweger.

And with special thanks to Brian Siberell.